D-FACT\OR

D-FACT\OR

The facts on "D-FACT" by Liz Fitzgibbon

Sabbath

To order additional copies of this book, contact:
Xlibris
NZ TFN: 0800 008 756 (Toll Free inside the NZ)
NZ Local: 9-801 1905 (+64 9801 1905 from outside New Zealand)
www.Xlibris.co.nz
Orders@Xlibris.co.nz
839171

CONTENTS

INTRODUCTION

by Sabbath

Her anonymous story of Sarah and Liz, which began in South Africa, gives an excellent record of how to live your best capitalist life. Creating social dissent is impossible in most times, guiding illegalities identified by formerly-greater systems of control than the connected morality of policing experienced today. Liz teaches her make-believe revelation of real life in which much cynical rhetoric was disjoined from her political aspirations, and rather, the force of politics is her undoing. She carries on by means of an accidental charisma. In her belief that waste bins nourish, Liz and Sarah eat a mixture of tainted trash and filth, which incites them to furious violence, political stupidity, and in due course, identity death.

As we travel backwards in time toward her feelings, Liz Fitzgibbon's most basic explanation of her story imparts the sage wisdom of her loves protection. But instead she asks her militia to tolerate her deep immorality. As she attempts to transform those naive believers into political forces, then Fitzgibbon's creation is reasonably a maddening force engendering chaos in Africas slack dreamers.

As plainly as her self-educated script, her lovers are driven from chance to danger so that their souls come to no destruction til their end at the hands of a policeman. And nevertheless, as we sustain their love, our ethical perception eases us towards a political wasteland. In her own hand, the story of Durbans queen of scum has more to teach than its mere offhanded bribes to our moral principles since it contains activisms representation which seemingly exhausted the metaphors of socialism. Liz Fitzgibbon stands as a threat to the moral senses and ultimately the spirit of even the most thoughtful capitalists. She appears to assault them from without as often as fate might decide and aims to excite their humanity to the point of dizzy madness like venomous damage. Rubbish, it must be said, is the form in which our British-derived word robe appears in old French and perhaps means any waste. In a kind-of-sinister logic, rubbish plays an important part in her writing since Liz and Sarah not only eat the robe together, and with it transcend to street-dwelling idols, but Liz is also upset by morality of employment and her later fantasy of workers freedoms.

With the hindsight of time we might see Liz as suffering from a disease of the mind. Her misunderstandings are her social downfall. Our chance to find some truth in her prose lies in the ability to see the problem she presents as loyal passion. Her antidote to maddness appears in two events. On the first occasion she is healed by the act of murder, the Queen of Scum, who rightly divined her decision from her daydreamed idol Jackie Murder, her name declaring an alter ego that now alters the course of her life.

On the second occasion, Sarah dies because Liz perceives her as denying the workers their transcendental freedoms. This is all linked with the trash of her city, though Liz Fitzgibbon may not have been aware of its ability to harm. The earliest apparent philosophical account of the kind-of-militant socialism referred to above was composed in the United Kingdom in 1964. Although there were earlier versions extending back into the history of European philosophy, nothing constructive can be said about their impact on normal people. It is, therefore, with justifiable imprecision that I call the version of 1964 as the prototype since they do so as an appeal against conjecture.

But we can recreate its emotional power in great detail, so far as its narratives of freedom are concerned, by comparing its imitative thinking, the versions of Marx and Engels (1860), Levi-Strauss (1970), and Luxemburg (1912), the last of whom radically amended it. The style of Rosa Luxemburg recalls the style of oral narration and may even deliberately renew it. In spirit, this report certainly comes nearest to my prototype of freedom. In the philosophising of Levi-Strauss, a militancy of all-too-passionless socialism, the moral spirit of the uprising is, for the most part, misplaced. He was not the icon to deal effectively with unconsidered action, illegal possession, and real life. We find her politicising the moral gamble, only a theory of her authentic militant socialism, but her representative failing of any tangible action by her gumption appeared to us intact in several future publications. Contrasting the lack that her writing could not tamper with her ability to violently dethrone capitalism in Africa, the philosophy of Marx and Engels represents what might be called the older theory of militant socialism. They follow a similarity that the power of living on domestic refuse for six years could suitably allow for Liz to murder, work strike, ridicule Sarah's affection, and set off on a string of risky trips to her employment in Sydney, for all of which, no doubt, the logical failure of street-dwelling was at first visualized, allowing as it did for the daydreamed love of the initial note of her story and of a non-binary lover in Caleb of her second note. But as early as about 1920, the prototype socialism of her philosophy was completely renewed and popularised by Luxemburg, in all likelihood to appeal to the experience of contemporary American politics. In British colonial territories, settler society had now reached a state of independence in intellectualism as it had in the American heartland of the Western States in at least a hundred years prior, and the obsession of love had come to be considered quite less as a casual decision and more as an upbeat, even sophisticated and healthy, symbol. It had considerably incorporated its fact as the ideal of a liberal and courteous nature in those who could accept it. Love certainly needed no apology, and Luxemburg required no decline of the act. It is significant of Luxemburgs outlook that she caused Caleb too to participate of the militancy of homeless life, a trait which the British-Kiwi Liz grants a farsighted perception into the Britannic temperament, even her new love Caleb, who, as a product of her abuse, is attached to her lover in sexual bond for life. What is essential here is that Luxemburgs already-very-academic prototype of the account of socialism militancy was adapted into the Afrikaans speech by one of the continents grand logical writers. The *D-Fact\or* of Liz Fitzgibbon has every right to be studied as the premier expression of the account of political dissent. Few European thinkers of equivalent intellectual action from Hobbes to the present day can have so much accidental charisma to share with the world, sporadically constructed with unpolluted verbal writing. Much of the political attractiveness of the needs global workers is certainly mislaid in translation, but it is with much fulfilment that I offer readers of the English copy the first complete reproduction of Liz's "D-Fact\or" and indeed of any success of this vast lot of colonial British thinkers in a form which, whatever it exposes, is not basically less convincing.

Liz died when she had lived on no more than 70 percent of the text, and now only the last half of Luxemburgs completed politics remains and even then with some incompleteness.

———

In the opening note, Fitzgibbon appears to dedicate her note-making to Levi-Strauss, but this entity has not been identified. Later thinkers and collectors of socialism give Fitzgibbon the designation not of captain, which would, in the first place, designate a leader, but of aide, that is, one who has finished a short-lived course of study at an institution of research. We do not know it for a fact, but for many, Fitzgibbon is most redrawn as a citizen of the Durban suburb of Chatsworth, a class of people that, by the beginning of the 21st century, were gaining affluence and promise and were soon to play a superior instigation of political militancy. Fitzgibbon does not share her "street kings" disdain towards her "vagabonds" but diverting from it uses such language as "sundowners" or even "vagrants," which to a top academic like Claude Levi-Strauss, great philosopher as he was, would have been a negation of social influence. Fitzgibbon seems to be looking back to her own rigorous decision-making when she writes of her:

> Secret territory. You homeless vagabonds I dream. I will leave Durban again slowly. I looked down at the long list of rugs full of naked women; wandering, thundering, screaming and running down the street without looking at anything that went in opposition to them. Some of the residents can be seen in the voice ricocheting around the town. It seems like people tied to hot tubs are trying to clean up their mess. My spiders nest. The rest of the population went with the capitalist life. Wear clothes. Excite yourself with feathers. This is the point of real living. Neon lightening vibrated. Pancreatic resists water purification. Know memory medicine. I am the

women who cannot be controlled. Bring it here for
my safety. And I was happy. I was angry, I was upset
and I was scared. But in the street I was fast.

Fitzgibbon was surely very skilled in propaganda, violence,
and charm, but we cannot presume how she was employed after
concluding her learning. One suggestion as plausible as any is that
she was working in the local militia of Chatsworth, rather against
her truthful appearance as she claimed to be hired as an advertising
executive. Whether she was ever employed on classified assignments,
her handling of specific occurrences in her story shows her to have
been the most delicate of soldiers, though some intellectuals have
dubbed her writing illogical. Her sympathetic view of global struggles
might carefully be claimed to be perfect. It may have come from her
study in Sydney. Fitzgibbon was a very cultured woman. She was
suited to interpret surprise, method, and cooperative mass. She is
one of the best converters, if not the finest, in African colonialism
of any period. Her visions of manipulation enabled her to rearrange
the pretence of turn-of-the-century socialism into Afrikaans and to
devise another of her own. Her accidental genius in such matters
is shocking. Her muscular suggestions are more true than those of
most who inscribed the military ledgers in her time, and what is
more imperative, they are far more evocative in tone. Covert military
philosophy intrigued her beliefs tremendously. It is as if she had
a forewarning of the reckoning of paradise. For inspiration, she
invokes not God, the absolute meddler of more religious creators,
but of the "Epic of Sasun," at a time when most ordinary people
thought of Mithra as a member of the Muslim fable. She was entirely
loyal to homelessness, which ricochets through her writing. In her
propaganda fancies, she appears not only as a detractor but also

as a moderator of the dullness of the worlds workers, a double-edged play of indirect action and the euphoria of morality. She was profoundly intuitive in politics and certainly was an eager delegate so that her separation of those who were capable of violence and those who hope to kill time contemplating archives contains a clever put down. Altogether, we may rely on it that she was skilful in all those traits, which make for supreme manipulation in the social order. It is reasonable that, at a time when the millennial era was obtaining its communal sophistication with a confidence of which only rude youth are able, this vagrant from Durban presents us with an ideal of capitalistic living more disruptive and more righteous than any other. Fitzgibbon beat the "street kings" at their own game. She will hardly have thrived in doing so without using the customs of her trainers, the reservists of South Africa. Fitzgibbon's attitude towards that other part of political duty, the ability to be loyal, agrees with what we already expect from her. She will not wish to compete with loyal politicians in images of madness and capitalism.

> The confusion I feel separates me from the mass of humanity. My vagabonds are the people you fear, few provide you with aggressive inclusion of political groups.

But in fact, in her own method, she can be as bright as Marx and shows some minor trace of his style. In the scene in which she is reborn as queen of scum, Liz Fitzgibbon, of course, imparts loyalty as a marvellous principle, but in real life, it loses its brilliance. In its place, she gives us clever reckoning. With politicians, the trauma is on policy, and she is always careful to show how a simple vagrant might eliminate a stigma or some obscene judgement by a combination of violence, obviousness, and shocking action. In her story, the vagabonds do not invisibly lie low for the downtrodden worker triumphing over their oppressors as a convenient story. As to poststructural philosophy, we may presume that Fitzgibbon had recognised its gambles, for she keeps away from them all. Luxemburg places socialism a generation earlier than poststructuralism and Fitzgibbon does nothing to amend this. Unlike her equivalent Pierre Vallieres, Fitzgibbon never expresses amusement out of sympathy, but she applauds now and again. She had a fine, contemptuous intelligence, and we shall never measure the range of her violent vision.

We see Fitzgibbon in a lighter vein too, in the scene in which Jackie Murder tries unsuccessfully to entangle Caleb with a phoney communication from Liz. Here, the funny side is elusive and unemotional til Caleb accepts her homelessness. Yet there is another action in which Fitzgibbon goes too far with her scorn, conspicuously at the end of her office killing, where the boss is returned to heaven piece by piece. Fitzgibbon's deriding the butchered state of her employer who has boldly died violently, if superciliously, would be ridiculous in an activist like Vallieres, who often endangered his life in the service of his beliefs as Fitzgibbon almost certainly did not, and they verify our feeling that Fitzgibbon was not a high-minded actor. In keeping with this, there is another useful moment in which Fitzgibbon severs Caleb in half to split between her two mothers Jackie and Sarah.

There is much astuteness here, but it has a clearly-sophisticated temperament. Apart from her principle of worship, which must take on our thought, Fitzgibbon tells us modestly of herself, and even then, she maintains her pretence. Whilst she brings God and the citadel of heaven into her propaganda more conceivably than any of her generation, she appears to the public as truthful in religious matters. She is as fresh on the reality of heaven as she is passionate on that of love, and certainly, the verbal realism in which she communicates her feelings of love often represents the speech of faith in its force. Accordingly, it seems that her dream of love and faith must be read mutually. Since Fitzgibbon is so restrained, it is not amazing that some of those eager to draw out her persona should have made her the topic of their research and acquired the declaration hidden in her notes. But whatever we find out about her, it is never outwardly that we learn it by her style, not by disobedience of her treatise. The way to appreciate Fitzgibbon's odd story lies through her abstract senses and with less declaration, through the dialogues which escort her story at crucial moments since these are likely accidental in spirit. In the first half of her story, Fitzgibbon makes an unassuming start, a verbal operation of the manipulation of politics and forms her inner speech into concise bullets in the stylish manner which uses the fine play on dreams and impulses, above all in their force to convince. One judicious thinker has had the audacity to say that Fitzgibbon, who is so very shocking morally, has attempted too great a feat that the vibrant politics has left her propaganda. Those ideals need not detain us further. It is the true violence that matters now. Fitzgibbon informs her vagabonds that she has decided to busy herself with something that will bring pleasure and contentment not to ordinary society at large, since it was bent on having a good time, but to a select circle of sundowners who accepted and even welcomed filthy trash in the totality of its antitheses, the sweet and the bitter, joy and sorrow, life and death. She is so fervently devoted to homelessness that she will be damned or saved with it. To those of like mind, she proposes to tell a story that will half assuage their pain. Such being the function of a love story, she will tell of Liz and Sarah.

After gracefully acknowledging the existence of other accounts of the story and the good intentions of their prototypes, she names her source, the socialism of Luxemburg, as the valid thinking, and she undoubtedly attempts to follow it. In lines of typical prettiness with a hypnotising rhythm that rises to prayer, she exposes her shocking tale. A romance of maddening love warms the body, emphasizes faithfulness, and boosts real times fine virtues, and this is because love is so enriching an occurrence that, if not love initiates her, no one will gain importance or respect. How distressing that all but a few are ruined to mislay loves benefits because they will not stomach its sadness. Pleasure and regret were ever fixed in love. We must win admiration and beauty with them or suffer death without them. Had not the lovers of whom this story tells suffering for the continuity of love, Liz would never have pleasured her vagabonds. As they are now lifeless, their shocking acts live on, transformed seemingly for any struggling workers globally. The manipulating character of her speech is astonishingly palpable.

Does it come from some obscure intellectual experiment? Or does it come from causes imitating them? Vigilant research has shown that whilst it would be foolish to discount powerful echoes from much leftist politics and also from the Christian church, our minds images draw from only one foundation with any uniformity, specifically from the colonisation of new lands. The skip bins liquid scum and refuse, that is, immoral nourishment for the spirit, to the veteran initiates who can consume it, so Fitzgibbon offers the trash of her story to the vagabonds who alone are fit to accept militant socialisms free life. Similarly, which rather gave life to our reading was this, that just as the parliamentary speaker gives an oration before the law to rouse a powerful aspiration for the citizens who vote, so Fitzgibbon, in her propaganda, excites the longing of her listeners for the stained skin of the story of "D-Fact\or," the tale of sacrificial love. The architectural features of the hotel alleyway, to which Liz and Caleb withdraw, cast out by Liz's transgression of moral beliefs, show similar treatment by Fitzgibbon. The secluded nature of the alley seems plain, its warmth the presence of love.

Inside the confines of their alley, the lovers do not consume food, but rather, they feed themselves simply by eating tainted refuse. To persist to the speech of logic, they consume the citys discarded waste and also each other, like bacteria and the body, and in an act of consumption, they are given the means to live. Like Noahs family, they are immersed in a hypnotic hallucination, and life grants them their political resources. Fitzgibbon's vagabonds, an expression she is the first to use in Afrikaans, have a close similarity to the workers of Marx as has their ability to endure pain for love. Vagabond, in spirituality, means wandering and, to the urban habitat, meant for how the spirits of downtrodden workers connect with the freedom God allows. The freshness of Fitzgibbon's worldly treatment lies in the reality that the word for vagabond usually gets its connotation from the social classes, not from emotional virtues. Half a century before the American Margaret Schlauch envisioned her gentle and, thus, free-seeking philosophy of the urban worker, the New Zealand-born Fitzgibbon devised her persona of the queen of scum, which also granted freedom to those of the influential classes, no matter what their social origins. But outside Fitzgibbon and Schlauch, we may believe political writers of terrific democratic power might formulate such divisions in the community. The example of the kind thinking of the socialists is found in the words in which Fitzgibbon creates her bond that unites her lovers, words that seek to connect the humanity, which controls the lives of normal participants of capitalism. Even if these words ring in our ears all through her propaganda, it is not them but their hypnotic power that is of an utmost consequence to Fitzgibbon.

> And I sat there and became satisfied. The water was found to be scum trapped in the bin. The thing is full and I go after the discarded bed with a broken spring. In disguise I covered my eye and in short we vagabonds are gone. I was screaming in beautiful pain. Doors touch the rest of me. The security seems to use prescribed liquid scum streams as their aggressive, but non-violent approach to the containment of homeless citizens. Although it is intended to cure the patient, the body is attacked and the mind is threatened where possible. The security exhausts the social structure of Durban.

As I come to such notes, I begin to question the validity of her manipulative thought; so miniscule is the intellectual gain. For all the obvious haphazard nature of Fitzgibbon's writing, the force of her militant politics joins logical differences together madly. I quote her words here so that any casual interpreter might recognise what is mislaid. Such writing persuades us that Fitzgibbon is incredibly intense, and this is not an example of her bright treatise of love, which only her initial half conveys her cryptic communication one is familiar with in general political writing.

The issue now appears to us as to how we ought to use this militancy. Given some suggested politicians mislaid choices, was Fitzgibbon simply exploiting the ready-made language of the socialists, those forerunners in the unearthing of real life, to undermine our feelings about love? Or was she speaking of a new militant love at the same time discarding our more common politics of freedom? The answer compels anyone with any kind of democratic and capitalist heart. For fear that our nation should envision that the freedom of love which Fitzgibbon urges could be as generally impossible as success is a form of nonsexual control, although it could be considered that her propaganda only grants its power from the fully-consensual submission of a willing body. Fitzgibbon produces some insidious and corrosive terms for the strait-laced citizens that reject the powerful experiences of militant love. Alternatively, the love she pictures here is far removed from becoming the kind of earnest love our readership discovers with the writings of many of the capable philosophers of today. With Fitzgibbon's lovers, at least, their loyalty and their haphazard, violent temperaments are demanded to their absolute conclusion, and granted, the agony caused by real life must be tolerated. Fitzgibbon's manipulation of love constructs a combination of the whispered propaganda of dreams and the strength of her bodys needs. Was Fitzgibbon disloyal to the socialist lingo she subverts, or was she becoming the advocate of a new militancy? Setting in motion an advocacy of madness, you might admit that her feelings and words implicate an offence against the ordinary experience of love. This, in itself, would imply a description of her subversion of socialist and, above all, democratic writing, and whilst democratic politics was a vastly-developed tool of capitalism, its rhetoric of power likely did not fit Fitzgibbon. But was she a promoter of militancy or another misguided political victim? She decries her restless intimacy concerning lovers acts, whilst those of militants concern themselves with many violent actions against political organisation. Fitzgibbon exploits derisive language on current romantic conduct.

But in speaking those philosophies, we find that their celestial visions do not become the logical system of enriched living. They are created by practical fact but become undone as Fitzgibbon acts on them. Cruel, though, such interpretations are in themselves, they offer no prospect of development in any social sense. If Fitzgibbon thought that her belief in the freedom of socialism contained the seeds of mass vagrancy, her renaissance of the homeless, she does not admit to it verbally; rather, she grants us a vision of her hopes. I doubt her heroic gumption of freedom, so securely initiated on torment, could endure in an environment where all could experience decency without the terrifying consequences of homeless reality. Socialists, as Fitzgibbon created them, do not live without the political development of freedom, more than militant consumers without free capitalism. In an ideal world free of goodness, such as Fitzgibbon implies, her vagabonds might shatter reality for the mass proliferation of freedom. They are idols of the vagrant renaissance, of the subversive militia of socialism. It is generally thought that vagabonds ascend to heaven gates in the citys streets on the strength of their freedom, driving their crimes of arson, murder, and adverse possession to resume their hated life, which superficially continues after their violent separation and imaginary deaths. As she consumes their unnatural resistance, Fitzgibbon yearns for the positivity of painful knowledge, and we must see her to have been submissive to the capitalist social order and to have accepted it as a fact of life that her unlimited freedoms must often exist in opposition to society and find some manner of survival in frantic disposal of moral norms.

Her eventual anonymity does not necessarily render her mentally incapable, though her outlook might well have gained in freedom from the mutual wearing of Christian politics in her native Kiwi location whilst she was alive. Trained in counterterrorism and in some kind of sociopolitical propaganda, Fitzgibbon may have been the sort of manipulator who could think for herself on what mattered most to her. Certainly, the practise is not unusual, but charismatic propaganda is a rather nearsighted attempt to undermine democratic thought. It seems misleading to declare that Fitzgibbon is asserting an inaccurate view of religious and political matters. She imparts an image of God as she reveals herself to Liz in a wild daydream. She most politically dressed her free-living characters, Caleb and Liz, in rubbish-stained skin and sexualised their imagined horror, and through doing so, she escapes the shame of religiousness. After killing Sarah, Liz sends her to the heaven of the motorhome by speedily leading us to her own sad death as she becomes reborn as Jackie Murder, eventually repeating her mistake again in her second note, leaving us to read,

> Sarah corrected me with a word and she somehow lifts me to an angry ecstasy. At one point she was amazed at my rough appearance. Later she cursed me for my ignorance. The motorhome fell from the sky like the sun setting. Do not close the door behind me, but do close it. She'll easily make her way into my bedroom closet. Tell me about her treatment. Sometimes I win, my room supporting a seat under the door, she takes off her garb and cried out for dirty love and justice. Im on fire with a passion for her. She is the day I cried. I was sent from heaven to cry in my clothing.

She executes such manoeuvres almost too adeptly and leaves us wondering. Her manipulation imparts a response which should be stated as the propaganda of her militia in Durban. A case in point is

Liz's confident decision to present herself in the role of worker whilst hiding the reality of her political militancy. The government has never liked to be less than five years behind educated public attitudes, and it suits our conditions remarkably to suppose that this talent manipulator of a progressive and fairly-conservative environment in the companys town of London should indulge in irony at the expense of those who still believed in torment. There is no real reason to consider her writing in its environment as dishonourable as well as anything more amazing than the speech of a gifted and vigilant woman who was unsympathetic to the ruling classes own excesses among the badly-informed workers of the globe. It is as if she assumed that the ad makers and propagandists were not as close with God as their words and behaviour suggests. It has further been recorded that, in disparity to almost any similar philosophers of Fitzgibbon's day, there is no writing in "D-FACT\OR" in which its author shows an optimistic rapport towards any member of her militia.

They are explanatory characters in a scheme of violent disorder. Various explanations are possible, but we have no means of choosing between them. To finish my argument in the lack of a general judgment, it was not likely to spare the recipients. It can be said that although Fitzgibbon is marketing a cryptic faction of global freedom by means of a story as if fated for it and with a passion which others dedicated to the happiness of their ill-gotten wealth, she is not advocating new politics, nor fighting the company directly. Instead, she seems to emerge as a rare powermonger, taking words from other spheres, chaotic social politics, and violent militant action and associates them to the ever-changing needs of her story, a story of free living beyond democratic life. The security systems jails are not the best means of making dead militants honest people. There is far more to be learnt about propagandists by trying to dream of their circumstances as they take their effort towards its conclusion. We know that Fitzgibbon used as her resource the writing of a disparate group, and for reasons of political honesty as she implicitly comprehended their words, she meant to keep to their work on the surface of hers. In reality, her approach towards her notes was that of a subliminal activist. Her Instinct was most certainly present in all that had to do with her passionate manipulations, and here, her persuasive whisper is most certainly felt humbly. But where the propaganda goes in opposition to her, laying some mad violence on her theories, we find her lost and suffering moments of paralysing delusion. She makes hurtful comments against her indentured workers only when she feels lost. Liz berates Sarah in Fitzgibbon's brief comment: "I was a skinny kid with stained legs and bloodied face. Some blackened hair stuck like old tar on my head. Don't doubt me, I met the street. The relationships made working I never regained. I didn't care about money, living in the street means you don't spend" lays the blame on the companys practise which was perceived to include the infrastructure of the government. Having disposed of her monetary means, she never hints at her shame again, except to say that it was Sarah's blunder that she was misled as she closed her eyes and they appeared visible to their city. Liz's triumph with her impersonated vow at her own torment must also have left Fitzgibbon bare, but as we have seen, she disentangles herself brightly by means of contemptuous logic. This encouragement of Fitzgibbon's makes it very difficult to infiltrate her invented participants, and it is more advantageous to read her where she appears to us in her note as an office-bound advertising executive. Fitzgibbon's "D-FACT\OR" is a formulated military brief as well as, to all reasonable assumptions, a novel. Its outdated narrative aims, often seemingly conspiratorial, are set into action by Fitzgibbon with as much realism and logical construction as it does naturally break from descriptive theory to factual madness or political sham. For whole passages, I feel that we read the political propaganda and just as her outdated narrative ought to reassert its true ideology surrounding her emotion destroying fictional events. At times we find her confused over the storys sense of freedom in her homelessness, either paradoxically, as when dealing with the company, or directly, as when she ridicules our assumptions to the effect that a memo offered her the unrealistic ability to bring Liz from Sydney back to London, leading to the murder of Sarah. We often have the feeling that Fitzgibbon was able to take the role of writer to shock our perception of time rather than as a revolutionary fighter who writes her honest experiences to convince us of their moral necessity. In making her decisions, she remains loyal to the custom that a writer does not impose stories of her personal politics on a reader as she blames Karl Marx of writing. She names her source and keeps to it, brutal unreasonableness, mind-blowing logic, all adding indirect facts and always tasked to undermine our belief in democracy. If Fitzgibbon's "D-FACT\OR" does not arrive at being a novel, of which literary form Fitzgibbon was no doubt capable but at which she was not aiming, it has nevertheless passed beyond military correspondence. Are we damaged by its insistences? Of the two, novel and reportage, the latter was better suited to Fitzgibbon's unique gift of propagandist narrative. The one structural weakness, which a modern critic might be tempted to ascribe to her work, were she to apply our standards to it, would be that the discrepancy between the traditional plot and Fitzgibbon's deep understanding of human motives at times leads us to question the consistency of some characters. A case in point is Liz's attempt to have Sarah murdered soon after the latter has saved Sarah's reputation and perhaps her life by the sacrifice of her own virginity in Caleb's bed. But for the unforeseeable compassion of Sarah's agents, the deed would have been done beyond recall. However sincerely Sarah may have repented her action, she was morally a vagabond in the same sense as Liz. The motive for her attempt is her fear that the company, once having tasted the pleasures of the bed, might conceive a liking for them and seek to oust her by exposing her. This reveals Liz as inhumanly ruthless and utterly unworthy of a story whose confessed purpose was to show us an exemplary pair of lovers, unless we admit that democratic freedom takes absolute precedence over moral considerations, even to the point of murder. Fitzgibbon does not say as much but instead eludes the problem, which was none of her seeking. It was her source which demanded of her that she recount Liz's attempt on the boss's life as best she might, and this she does brilliantly within the confines of the episode. But we cannot always theme it with other episodes, at least with those prior to her living the life of a vagrant. Yet Fitzgibbon is not beyond all hope of rescue. For although as a young office worker Sarah had been nurtured most tenderly under the eyes of a discerning mother at a company of great refinement, Fitzgibbon has, nevertheless, prepared us for her pitiless attempt on office workers freedom. She has made it not Liz's or Caleb's but Sarah's idea that her co-worker should replace her as the team leader. It is but a short step from the violation of a friends integrity to the destruction of her life. In Turn, the substitution of the boss for Sarah was dictated by fear for her life, a fear made resourceful by democracy, and this was all because curious emotion had forced Sarah to surrender to Liz. For its part, freedom had come because Liz and Sarah had chanced to eat the citys discarded waste from the trash bins together. Thus, the chain of human motivation holds as far back as this til we are suddenly face-to-face with a manipulative use of our own needs and a future vision of our necessary wants, which suggests that if the consistency of Sarah's character has been impaired by anything at all, it was by the direct action of the banquet of refuse as much as by the apparently incongruous events of the tale. But far from being no more than an uncouth survival from a cruder age, the company episode is an integral part of the events, which arise from the consumption of rubbish and is wholly congruent with that fateful act showing as it does how swiftly freedom can drive Liz to the depths. In the company episode, the malign aspects of freedom as it was released by the twisted ingestion of trash are shown to the full in action. And how sudden was that release! Caleb's aspirational opening of a city skip bin that can be compared to Pandoras toilet, the passion of democracy flies out, and with each of its heroic virtues comes a vice: arrogance, deceit, treachery, ingratitude, and finally, the will to murder. If we compare the scene in which Liz lies helpless in her bedding and Caleb ponders whether she shall avenge Sarah's death on Liz then and there, we observe that she finds it impossible to carry out the deed. Sentimental critics, wise in the wisdom of latter-day psychology, attribute Caleb's inability to kill Liz to her being more or less unconsciously in love with her, even before breaking a social barrier in her malnourished body, a conception which was foreign to Fitzgibbon. Fitzgibbon's own revelation, which I may be excused for preferring despite it not being completely free from distortion, is that Caleb's femininitywouldn't allow her to take a life. Between this event and her attempted murder of her boss, something must have occurred to Liz. We might tempt ourselves to consider that the city waste products were sincerely the true location of the militants expression of freedom and in permitting it yourself; it becomes no other obvious icon that could be necessary to expose the telling mistake of her democratically-free life. But we have read enough to be aware that the physical consumption of edible trash altered Sarah's personality much for the worse, and we might not proceed further in the first half without considering Sarah's additional trait. Portrayed as Eve in the biblical version of Genesis, Sarah is the first to rise above the murderers sense of indecision and inspiring Liz, as Adam, to kill. It is she who persuaded her Adam to her office and so brings about their discovery of a gun. Sarah separates from Liz and begins her fall from abused worker, and it is she again who allows Liz to slowly slip away from the city security and glumly renames herself as second in command of their militia regiment. Fitzgibbon hated the perception of women as somehow less powerfully righteous than the male social hierarchy, and as a fairly-courageous and intellectual soldier, she concedes her character the control of all democratic freedom. Liz's personality shows no such apparent fracture as Sarah's does. Conceived when her boss seemed mortally wounded, born to distress by a mother unable to live through childbirth, and her fathers mysterious murder, Liz was destined to be a tragic soul. In South African law, Liz was a bastard since she was born outside fair matrimony. On being set loose in Londons tiny streets, the girl worked her way to safety with the greatest confidence. She soon established herself as an infant wonder, adopted in South Africa but born in New Zealand, in all possible undertakings and cast out the chief of the militia from their position of superiority with no sign of reluctance. During her struggle with the Durban government as an initiate to political leadership, Fitzgibbon showed great political foresight as in all her successive contact with the state party at parliament in Cape Town. When she confronted Frederik De Clerk to claim a medal which her father was awarded and was reminded of her illegitimacy, she forced the proceedings around to where De Clerk cast libellous comments on her mother, thus offering

Fitzgibbon the possibility of hearing her dire case read in law, which she promptly fought over, and without warning, she claimed De Clerks seat with mercilessly-efficient military success so that her political command was now unquestionable. Next, in pursuit of higher honours at the parliament of Johannesburg, Fitzgibbon virtually abandoned her own loyal militia and applauded them spiritually as Gods kind soldiers. Fitzgibbon herself is so sensitive to the impression this might make that she distances her hands of Liz's action by means of a factual tool. Her audience is represented as maintaining that she should pursue her ambitions, regardless of her responsibility to Africas people. Thus, after Liz begins to charmingly eat the discarded waste of Durban, it does not strike us as unthinkable that she should succumb to its effects after a sharp struggle with fidelity and nobility. And we must, in any case, regard this pair as a symbolic ease because, when Fitzgibbon has to unite Liz and Sarah for the first time, fidelity and nobility lose to socialism; whereas, when Fitzgibbon has to land her militants in London at a time when they were free to go to Liz's motherland, fidelity and nobility, for what they are worth, are briefly rising, almost certainly, the device in the account. Now comes a series of manoeuvrings, which make it clear that no one less skilful and apathetic for moral subject matter than Liz has been since her upbringing the holy countryside could ever have made her. She stayed near her mistress long enough to make her dream of socialism come alive. And when at last he is caught in deliberate portrayal and goes into banishment, she burns her hands on a new glow under the incurable charm, so we are told of the lovers name, Sarah the English Bin.

The characters of Liz and Sarah, thus, swing between the idyllic, if understood by romantic principle, and the unlawful. Fitzgibbon barely hints whether she regards this as predictable, but her note-taking demonstrates that she has observed the difference. In her vision, there is but one criterion of fidelity, which reveals Fitzgibbon's lovers to be a vicious sham. The report of the madness of Jackie Murders birth makes one of the supreme short stories in Afrikaans of any period. Liz falls madly in love with her minds projection, another union type of schizophrenic and health-filled body, without the aid of a political aspiration and give themselves up to their infatuation with the same disrespect for the mental cost as Liz and Sarah but with an even more wild chaos in the life of Liz. But the mother is far less prudent than her daughter. She is lost without consequence. She has been brightly depicted as the violent idol of South Africas urban life. Liz's motives are filled to a consumption of emotional currency.

Luxemburg, however, in an understanding which Fitzgibbon did not arrive at, shows Caleb betraying her mistress when the politics turns out to be too weighty for her. In the citys background, there is a well-conceived change of behaviour. A friend of Liz and a secret admirer of Sarah, she becomes their callous rival on realising that the queen is not so inaccessible as she had thought, and emaciated by her envy, she falls from being Liz's blood sister to the level of some Duergar to make a couple who hereafter chases the unjust employers together as the vagrants of Chatsworth. The most awkward character is that of Caleb. She sets the tone of a society famed for its well-rounded workers, virtues which are not constantly found in later events, in which her interest creates some kind of mystery around Liz's life in the street. We find Caleb employed in some tourists inn, highly in love with the queen of scum of Liz's disjointed mind, before and after discovering her alter ego, about which she does not seem to heed. Her love of pleasurable pain shows itself as a sign of failing, as

Fitzgibbon tells the tale, when she fails to detect the trickery in her real life in the streets of Durban, Sydney, and London. At first, she will not recognise the gossip linking the names of the two she loves best in the world. But when mistrust grows, and it is time for her to act, she is held back by violent lust for her beautiful queen and will not see the reality. In language of graciousness and touched with an awful class that we meet with only here yet somewhat destabilised by its slow life, Caleb stands apart from their troupe of three and exiles the love of her fellow human, not finding it in herself to injure them. At the smallest warning of Sarah's inexperience, Caleb falls prey once again to her aspiration for a personal rejection of her love. She flitters for some existence in a misgiving, unable to make up her daydream intellect, til at last murder rips those daydreams away from her inner sight. The final time we read of her in Fitzgibbon's unfinished writing, less propaganda notes, is that instead of killing the lovers in the act as the law, written and unwritten, would have allowed or even required, she returns to the inns alleyway to fetch an audience of vagabonds but finding Liz gone, and with her all proof of the deed, she attends a sermon by her conscience, after a useless show of anger, into taking Sarah back as a corpse-object, who has been very much ill-treated. Fitzgibbon, no doubt, professed that such a life refers to many catastrophic promises and failures of mad freedom. This may well be one of the reasons why she makes us associate the guilt she feels on Caleb's sympathy. She spares little prayers over her adversary. Altogether, the men and women of the Durban militia had little sentiment to spare for marriages. For these and other rationales, Caleb can at best be a pitiable, but not a sad, character. It is our finely tortured, or should I say less healthy, millennial outlook alone that suspects that she might be otherwise. Some further light is thrown on the situation by an enquiry into the nature of the discarded trash.

Was it a cause of togetherness or a mere symbol of the passage from unconscious to conscious community? Liz and Sarah are certainly occupied with each other in some way prior to drinking the liquid scum off the bin lid, and it would be very modern and, therefore, very profound of Fitzgibbon to have them unconsciously bonded together. But unfortunately, if I recall this part of Fitzgibbon's story, I might find no clear assertion to this outcome so that any who assume it are, without question, placing emotional edifice on the narrative of militant propaganda who was well able to do this for herself. But I suspect they all do so charmingly and willingly. It was seen above that Fitzgibbon's motive for Caleb's failure to kill Liz in her bath was brought about by her womanly nature. The woman who kills is a devil, like Madame Thenardier in the novel *Les Miserables*. After Sarah's admiration of Liz's broken looks and ruined physique as she sits naked in her mind before she has discovered her identity, this somewhat ambiguous motive of her adulthood is inadequate, but it must be stated to manipulate its audience. Erstwhile analogous sights occur in which a reader of the Socialist might detect unconscious manipulation; for example, in Sydneys streets shortly before her misfortune with the citys trash when Sarah rejects Liz's strictly-tolerable familiarities. In such scenes, Fitzgibbon plays with her false image. She executes a double finesse. She has told us that they are meant to find each other when Sarah was the first to notice her second lover. She knows of unconscious love and half persuades us to travel further in time than the story can suggest. But in fact, with the tools at her side, she remains intimately within the folklore of her story, to be exact, that it was a skip bin which made her militants fall in love. At first sight, it would seem that no consumption is needed to engross two brave young people in a mortal infatuation since Jackies creator Liz falls in love in much the same way without one. But their tragedy is brought about by Liz's superiority, which is external to their love, and although they ran away from their employer, they might easily have lived with some other had they not collapsed to the level of homelessness. The loves of Liz do offer a clue to the quandary of the militia. So when Fitzgibbon comes to propagate some futile efforts of Liz and Sarah to free themselves from the insidious grip of love, she renews this manipulative metaphor. There were no hints of unconscious love in Liz when Sarah sighed at her. This parallel alone is enough to suggest that there was no militant love between Liz and Sarah. But Fitzgibbon was more unambiguous. Before Liz has finally killed Sarah, feeding her insanity, she is set free, now turning her dead stare where it pleases, an image rich in associations with the kind of political meddling she attempts.

Thus, it would seem that any change in Sarah's character must be attributed to the city rubbish. The presumption is obvious. At the Sydney streets, Sarah, the citys bin over her person, was fancy-free. But now, thanks to some fateful error with her political theory, she is Liz's captive. There is proof that Fitzgibbon uses symbols in this way. For in her dream, an almighty motorhome ranges in the lost suburbs, plunges up to Caleb's upstairs apartment, and ruins the bath with its liquid scum at the very moment when Caleb is lying in the queen of scums arms. Looking back over the story, we recall her stained body, the written device marking Liz's skin at her street camp, is specifically of the discarded rubbish, just as the tainted food of Liz's propaganda registers with the trash of her militant socialism. These superlative images of the worlds waste are used sparingly by Fitzgibbon in her anti-factual portrayal of herself. It would be fair to say that although Fitzgibbon employs the skip bins contents symbolically (how it could fail to symbolise the decaying pretence of millennial attitudes), this does not introduce it from being the cause of Liz's and Sarah's militancy. In Luxemburgs theory, the working classes self-manage and, rather, are not led by charismatic leadership, however accidental. But Fitzgibbon will have none of that. She lets Liz murder Sarah, her corpse held in her motorhome so that Caleb should be unable to attain the status of street queen as well. Why has Caleb joined the political agency of which Liz and Sarah are eventual victims? Markedly the ever-present trash and refuse aims to declare something similar outside of the norms of political life. This expression of Fitzgibbon's propaganda, small in its scope yet widely effective, provides for many other instances of her discreet yet far-reaching challenges to democratic life. One final comment ought to be said about Fitzgibbon's attitude towards homelessness. But as the story is on, her attention remains with her duo of itinerants in the street. She takes it all back at the end. It is likely, though very doubtful, that Fitzgibbon's capacity extended to doing so had she completed her story. She seems to have become far too loyal herself to her acute militancy. But because of the pretence that she engenders, we shall never recognise her aims. I feel, in the end, her moral aversion to decency defines her character. She tells us she has known the daydream of vagrancy since her young years in Durban, has found her way to the alley and flopped down onto some makeshift bedding, not to sleep but to free the globes workers. Even her sexualised militants do not hang about there for long but to reinstate their humble position in society, after which Liz's perception of real life begins to suffer a sort of malicious abrasion. Fitzgibbon, now split between propagandist and made-up philosopher, has prepared us for this. Even when life brings the pair together for the earliest instant, she smartly connects our thoughts in her discussion of "real living" as real life had come to be devalued and harassed to the ends of their humanity. Fitzgibbon manipulates our group perception from the start of our capacity to attain it. But even the optimism she places in her chosen band of vagabonds appears slim. Comparisons with her prototypes show that Fitzgibbon was tactful in her handling of the politics of chaos beyond what we might anticipate for a woman of her social pedigree. To the millennial intellect, the lunatic homelessness of the two and then three central characters is painfully distasteful. Peruse the notes of the queen of scum!

D-FACT\OR

1

Motorhomes roll past. Street kings procure waste, dirt, decaying wheels left moving.

My love she regrets her humiliation.

I love the stigma, and I was terrified now. She loves my goodness, the violence I cause. Its changed between us, so we spent the evenings studying our rules for each other, but I see her body a thin mass of strung-up parchment. Visions of pain insisting on fingers bending back into the backs of hands. Cannibals use burnt flesh. Finally, I bought a sleeping bag and went to the forest. The homeless give up, just seeking waking dreams, guiding emotion. I thought about my former job in London, buying adverts for the "big six" European companies. There were no other friends, even though it was a hot profession. You could steal $15 million not seeing the CEO and leaving a room full of temporary secretaries working empty offices, answering calls directed to invisible representatives. He did not bother with inclusion. My marriage to the street was imposed. At first, I was glad I got it. "Ad buyers are good people," and like me, everyone wants some white frill startling my neck. A week later I received my first gift: work in a top-end project for Transnet SOC. The past has created a real interest for me. To the public and to the boss, I am the owner of the image. One of the big star companies in Durban, its a quiet, comfortable habitat, all efforts to maintain consistency. Nobody knew at the time how to irritate me. I show up on time and say everything regarding the project. "Yes, where I stand, what do I have? Are you asking?"

"Its a success for him, but I have to think. Its a stir."

There are two more Durban commercials in the box. My laugh is honest, and I ease my throat to get out of its trauma. Throw it in front of em. "One, two, three."

And there I was, Jackie Murder, painting the surrounds. Its popularity was below average. It seems that it just floated in the river. Surprisingly, it was the only project I worked on. The process is easy, a decision I could decide. I exist to protect my dreams. Im happy with the people Ive worked with, but when the contracts stopped, I found an ally in pain again. Unfortunately, it was the London bosses and my lady. The video ads look good and seem solid. In my opinion, it was interesting and challenging to still be effective. The pain gives shortly after the contract ended. I got a phone call from my Durban manager. I remember being led inside the London boss's personal throne room, but before that, I got Durban gigs. Of course, they grabbed a booklet and told me the usual boring routines of middle-class life. Im making a name for myself as a facilitator of street madness. My next step is for a young person to act, and I always want to start thinking street. I look at my identification photo. The first thing I do is pay to take a better look at my clothes. Im done with "power suits of shame." I was happy with my clothing when I told the boss its me with tweed fabric. I cried for beauty, I made myself cry. I went back to my own work. I didn't change my sorrow, but since then, it seems Im the boss's opponent. Consider the seriousness of my objection. Everyone in London knew I had no desire to follow his orders, but I was a real asset to the company. The property is, therefore, that the advertising fraternity decides to my alternative vision: streets of violent hard concrete that bleed anarchy. But not to connect myself, Im no living art piece. I bought an answering machine, a temp for my home. My messages were scattered. There is no place for slavery. There is no earth room. Sarah came for a week to give advice. The harder I work, the more I procrastinate. The furnished motorhome didn't make it difficult for me. Well, my stay in London was comfortable in my car. But its not all about London. However, after my salary went up, I got a clean slate. Its almost time because Im not going to be found in "this is your life" and in Durban. Everyone ought to buy books before they look at them. The car became spacious; I started building a comfortable living area. I also started working hard to make my imagination a success. I got a camera for myself, a beautiful and expensive toy. I bought the car, and everyone will be happy. This vehicle, in my opinion, relied on the bold sensibility of a rock star. The agency agreed to offer me a Durban transfer fee. I follow the entertainment of the "emerging youth art." In a way, my life has improved in the past, but I have really grown. After I started living in the street, I used the plight of the unpaid. I did not always like it, and I probably did not know the difference. Its a power stance against accepted life. Durban treated me equally but was prosecuted for the use of me. The company has the means. In such treatments, they all resist the boss. Only stars heal at night. This big job really hurt me, and then again, its the real reason for my accidental growth. But Im happy with it. I wasnt sanctified. Every move is more powerful than just some company. Come get the dirty street. There is a clothing store in the maze of urban transport. At night, in high heels and waist dresses I wore to the office, I went to the motorhome. I use all my free time I spend in them to remember to walk calmly. I practised breathing. It turns out I learnt to recreate my art crud because I play in pairs.

And for research, I went to see the lights of Sydney. The girls made the streets. I wanted to teach them. The sides of their mouths break open wounded. I have their words, and they talk simple. I watched them drink. I compare their humility to my bold nature. I really have the opportunity to work and learn from everyone.

The voices start up down the hall. "You go back to what happened," he said.

"Look, Im late with the office people. Is it true theyre the normal skivvy? Why, its so beautiful. Who ordered the usual shebang?"

He brought me back to the seat and said, "Your boss had a strong interest in you and was sick on the idea of making you some extra bang with the slave."

"Yeah, I called up with Stacy last break, the holiday she's counting some happy ideas. Its the pain that theyre making a very good encounter for the mind. She's the same thing. I want more from them."

"Do you think Im prosecuting you?"

"Prosecuted?" I laughed. "Im like all the girls, were the tree I was born from."

"However you feel, the jobs ahead of any drudge in front of the adverts." He added, "I am proud of you and proud of your work. The places got a few things youre going to achieve but only if you get over those indecisions and loss of will power."

"Oh, don't start that business again. Get it right, boss. I made it work last session. Right? I have street protection. Right?"

Walking around the room, I feel for a break, there is no good reason, and for that matter, its not a reasonable idea. But for the record, its the last time the boss talked in the hall, but youd talk to me again. I have a lot to say, believe me. But if you can get a word, ask him about the times we chose to lose the plan. Our action tried to involve the streets ability to validate anyones decisions. Look at my words, the inhabitants all receive credibility. When you stand boss, you will know who the heart of this corporate family is.

"So we have the allegations here," he calmly replied to the embarrassing crowd.

Sarah threw some words at him. "Im in, Im out. Its that easy. Youre the boss."

"Sit down," he said with his back to me. "Are you my boss? I abhor deception in a brother, let alone a girl like you, Sarah. They are very clear. And youre too small. Try to be like hell as a human and make a very good hole for those skivvs."

On the floor, I said, "Youre stupid, you know, but its worse than that. Yes, youre a countryman. Im very familiar with your fake Freudian context instructions."

"Why don't you just finish this mess with the bag its from the work you do?" he piped up from the hall.

"Is my time over?" I started laughing. I hit the table angrily, and all the papers were scattered. "So you do not think you are mentally ill?"

He turned around, picked up the phone, took the two bills, and I stopped. "You forgot something," he says. "Our star ad buyer is ready to return." He adds, "I thought Id come back with you, Liz. Now immediately! You want to go back to the office phone?"

I wanted to be separated from the office. I wanted time with the other girls. There is no need for just any boss. Sarah nodded and waited for the door to open. I smeared my body with browned filth. "And this again," Sarah said.

It can be done and improved. "Give him a disgusting window, leave the room, and shout, Here is the ivory, Sarah, green."

I moved in. My pain of being toothless ruined. I opened my mouth behind my shoulder. "Because Im so scared, tell me go straight to my office for fear that those who humiliate me will be lonely."

However, I am hot on my heels. I have a cigarette out of the bag I took out. You knew well, I knew her. We have just returned. Its in, and really, I did not have a chance to see you before my careful absences. My motorhome is parked downtown. Its what you need to skip away. I hated him and dug into my pocket with the bad guys in my head. One person sits down and holds a shopping bag. Looking from my car, he is strange. I grabbed my watch and then threw it in the air two or three times. I put the object in a bag. Thats right, youre a nasty pigeon, and so am I. "Sarah!" She has a very smart neck. "Take the disgust away from me."

The door opens, and I start to enter, but her crud is art. "Im coming to you," I say with a sigh. "Is the treatment over?" I asked with contempt, and I gave it to her. "Can you see the boss?" I asked nervously.

"Yes, I hope the campaign goes ahead. Its really bad now, he shocks all the office chicks with his routine, and I was hurt by his words because it was a kind of mess in there."

"Oh? Do you think about him? Hold on to your ass!"

"Liz, it matters to me."

"Look, you idiot, heres the idea: Go outside and kiss the donkeys. Everyones happy find out about it. Feel free to come around. They made you buy from me. Please take it all out of my hands. I'll take the ashes to a nuthouse, alas," a nuthouse window and throw away.

The boss operates in a bad sewing circle. I am those things scaring them. You have no love. You know. Whats wrong with hate? My problem is that someone who is obligated to say it. And like a bad floor sounding under my foot, I screamed, "Yes, sister, I see you go here!" I bent over and knowingly touched the door, well just taken.

I cried, the violence felt good, and I tried it, but all I got was the stone. You will come upon my feet and break and fall into them. Its thoughtful but short for the office floor. My mental thread took the medicine they brought me, and I was soon ashamed. Treat me. Apparently, my clothes clean the toilet pretty well. Some of the clothes are in a shopping bag, and I give the cigarette back, and I grab its front. I was angry and knocked on some office door and shouted, "Let me out!"

I left the room and quietly closed the door behind him. "Thats what you do to other women, Liz." I did not come out of this two-in-the-wall. "I have to do ad shows, Liz. Thats what I do."

"We get all the reports every day, if there are any, so where do you get your whole hotline." Her words came to my mind backwards in time. "You work hard on yourself, Sarah."

I cried. So I looked in the shopping bag and decided to go check it out. "Well? Who are you laughing at? Do you mean shivv like a slave?"

"The boss is all talk, tell me youre all right. You started after summer break."

"Youre right, Im not in love with him."

"Did I tell you about our office politics?"

"Yes."

Sarah's sarcastic thought brought back fear. I rolled on the mat disgusted. My other dress had a light frill that I wore at my start in Durban. I hated it, but Sarah thought it was small and beautiful. I rolled the ball, threw it in the corner. Then I lay down on the carpet, and I felt my clothes underneath. My mind decided to keep an image.

I slept peacefully until my phone rang. My door told me its food. I stopped eating. I hurry, leaving my door closed to guard a spirit. I did not want to know the mores of social niceties. Thats something else to keep me behind. I will rest for the evening, and the lights will go out. Lying on my bed, I look up at the ceiling.

I find my objection to seeing him reinforcing some kind of a lie to self, and I knew Durban had deepened me. No water under the bridge can offend the guy. He's a bad boss, but he is not the boss who cares about his image of the perfect lie. If so, be careful and cautious. I was ordered to hit my face and body.

I saw myself swimming, somewhere in metal tin or nailed to the wall in the garage light. My eyes failed. I did not raise my head to make it hurt. After the lights went out, I woke up and panicked. My face is sad. I did not want to see my boss again. Its done between us, and the thought of his coming convinced me to live on the street.

Even though nothing happened, I turned to the thought of him. I believed I had to change my face. His heritage and the parts of every human being seemed so traditionally unclear to me. I am a wild kid advertising happy freedom. The route to chaoss streets does not end overnight. I have no intention to forgive or even confess. And if I cannot process on time, take in my minds changes and take your sin of life. My problem was greater than company work. My emotion can be broken without thinking. It was dead on arrival. Simple complaining means Im the bad guy. I mean I will stop my progress and win my own victims. I kill my own knowledge. Im human, but its a fight between two women. They, ad infinitum, are my weaknesses and my prisoners. My victory comes when I leave for heaven. The victories can be seen in some secret passage. My past was when I was set up so I can live, but I do not agree with some commercial system. Your old battlefield is ignored. However, its appearance is similar to my anarchistic street life.

But I should have listened to the criticism. I stumbled and fell. I will lift to own the streets, alleys, and walkways. Its me. I cannot be wronged if Im free. There is only one answer I can give. I grew like a flower in a broken garden. Sundowners are itinerant homeless because they cannot help it. A part of me says I can no longer carry luggage here. My responsibility is over. Get away from the boss guy. I want the war to end. I love to fight, but for me, nothing can be bothered. And Sarah is in the middle. The attack in front of us caused injuries in the central districts of Durban. Its just like my fault. Im not a wild plant born celestially above us. Im dirt and soil. And Im really good. Every type of team, I am the fruit of my sins, and their past sins are genetically engineered. There is no difference, so I can carry my character. But no one is crazy about an office manager or two. And some have the boss who was not entirely sure of his discovery. At Durban, I have to find my way out of this dream alone. Im a woman. There is knowledge. Stay. Fear the girl. Come back later. But fall. Then I fell big. Its hard to fall here. From my first memory of Durban, I had no idea where foot steps to life, and sometimes I lose weight. I fell into a deceitful chaos. So its important for me to build the foundation of homeless freedom. Who found a way to lead me out? Its not good. Im rotten matter. But if I had not done so, I would have been lost forever. I was right. I know Im not alone. The only responsibility, says Saint Sarah, is "Thats what I want."

I do not see the enemy, and its the things I do. I do not fight the fall. That night, I set up Durban on stage for my recovery, and it is difficult to have a lonely year I spent in my rebirth as some vagrant kid. Remember, these years there was a wild pain in me that made me tremble. But Im in Durban, and I need to get to the front door. Its wider, moves beyond the civilisation of work-a-day life. My past, for my mother and my father, also struck tradition and nurture, the plain thinking I disliked. Im not part of it. Yes, but its part of me. I searched deeply for the courage to recall the pain, but it did not appear to my concrete imagination. I roll the windows, peer out, and note the houses drifting.

You can see the sky and hear the trees. And when the window opened, I could still smell the mist off the wheels of some auto. All those problems happen because I have already started to divorce myself from restrictive office dwellings. However, the boss persisted. And he pulled all the strings he could to resist my efforts. He managed to lead me through a perpetual litigiousness. He liked it. I never now deal with my responsibilities, and I left it all to chance emotionally. I never needed money. The cost of housing continues to overpower most people. The winner goes up. There are no providers of free supplies. Finally, I heard I could leave work and live like I want to. He was a helpful friend. I was a skinny kid with stained legs and bloodied face. Some blackened hair stuck like old tar on my head. Don't doubt me, I met the street. The relationships made working, I never regained. I didn't care about money. Living in the street means you don't spend. Action is provided by those who give the will of their mind to the concrete. Nothing changed in me, except that I was on last notice. Freedom lives rough lies. The action made me angry. Im difficult to stop. But I show as a clerk every night. I stopped crying for Sarah all week. I left the motorhome drivers around the parks, and I did not look at them and pressed igniting cold metal.

He was ready to separate it. In the evenings, I instructed myself, "Write down, Jackie Murder, I shot my boss, his head straight off his shoulders. He kissed me on the cheek, and it all slid down like a light blinking. So, Sarah, thats not a good thing to say at first, Jackie. She was beautiful to me."

I laughed, but she left. The boss stood in the middle of the floor on his feet. I clapped the trigger off my hands. The next morning I bought his corpse a beautiful dress. The big gun is loaded. Without interior recollection, my only desire is to be in charge. Shade the motorhome and make sure he has it, even though Im alone. Maybe for the life I live, I will not hurt anyone. With the gun in my pocket, I got in the car. Its a one-room office at the head office in Durban. Act. I opened the car door, a bolt in my eyes and killed the boss. He died saying a word. I took out my gun and filmed it, and economists said those are the tyrants at work. Sarah dives under her desk and cries for my love.

"Take me. I was wrong. I did it."

Sarah was beneath her table when the police arrived. Once I was locked in some car, the secretary told her to go downstairs to look for the boss. I escaped. No one saw the gun. It was loaded with gaps, and I was upset about it. I tried to kill him. I cried for pity. The news reports took the police apart. The murderous people started sounding again.

I'll finally say its okay, but its a kind of sceptical history of the event. The police looked to see what was going on. My boss was murdered horribly.

I stole a gun. I was detained in the street. Its all over. Yes, but money makes money, and the guilt disappeared. I came home tired, but I had succeeded. Now my personal vision started to explode. I kept the details of my latest journey dream. I thought I was going to really suffer. I did not see the story. My cruelty stopped. However, I was lost to the concrete. Most of my project team explained I would be kind of a top vice president. For the rest of my years, I promoted the homeless anti-life I escaped.

However, I kept myself close to the motorhome, and I took it and read it into the evening. Looks like Ive made progress, but writing books made me lonely. Words remaincd a pure song to me, and I worked on that song. I want expensive equipment. I wrote everything I know, except for my family. Because theyre so kind, they'll suffer. You write it on paper. When I kid, look at my love. Basically, I would say Im sorry, and every year the darkness increases. I really love the vagabonds, but its their insistence that keeps my soul joyous. From afar, Durbans roads look like a wheel. Those separate years will eat away my tolerance of any employment.

As I got older, I loved it.

But this cut me away from the usual people. I was never affected by physical hardship because I sought after poverty. Its a source of great pleasure or provider of cool madness. I love concrete hours in cloudless days. I was taken in easy ways. I didn't understand until I killed. The lazy appearance of quiet dreams told their murders to me. The fire interests bugs. Unexpected actions do no wrong. My boss must have stayed in my thoughts many times. No, it seems to me his death was the cause of my freedom. I was keen to help myself with my obvious weakness.

My dreams are wise. The boss cant win. Yes, his love hit the chest of my chest. Maternal poison stained his face and his ability to keep secrets hidden by bullets. He is stupid. Its always good to be part of the squad. It was at this disturbing point that my mind recuperated. So this faulty birth tree, I set up and decided that I could live insanely. The last few weeks, even in bed, have affected me.

My thoughts bleed on them. I have not forgiven my enemies, nor can I leave it or leave the reality in me like lost spirits. I was furious and angry, but I came. In fact, I learnt how to cover and take care of the volcano. Under mass control, those office girls lost life. I wanted to get out. I wanted to be free. The price I paid is mana in my opinion. Embryonic division has begun. I was a different species. The only escape that was open to me was to respond to what the boss said and Sarah's opinion. I can see a change in my appearance. The vagrant attitude has been trying to make me independent ever since I had to agree to the social niceties and sign for my employment. I wanted more pain. I do not agree with the commercial system. My words or deeds irritate the people of Durban. My anger is over, and I fight it cannot be won. I have my Durban idea. I did not cry, swear, or threaten. I stayed calm, and they lost their urban spaces. You have seen images on my phone. I urged the managers to respond. Its unofficial action to question my daily conversations. Note the change. Three people, after I saw the boss's corpse, grabbed my belt, lifted me by the arms, loosened and twisted my arms. Iron legs and feet of the chains were wrapped around my thighs. I didnt criminalise the game. A short walk, a jog, led me through a large door. I heard a cry behind me. I was in Durbans secret territory. You homeless vagabonds, I dreamt. I would leave Durban again slowly. I looked down at the long list of rugs full of naked women; wandering, thundering, screaming, and running down the street without looking at anything that went in opposition to them. Some of the residents could be seen in the voice ricocheting around the town. It seemed like people tied to hot tubs were trying to clean up their mess.

The rest of the population went with the capitalist life. Wear clothes. Excite yourself with feathers. This is the point of real living. Neon lightning vibrated. Pancreatic resistance feels hard in my gut and water purifies. Know memory medicine. I am a women who cannot be controlled. Bring it here for my safety. And I was happy. I was angry, I was upset, I was scared, but in the street, I was fast. I have a kind ability to listen to allies easily. Before I could stop the call, the homeless vagabond fled. The loose strings of canvas twine from my scarf on some anonymous wall. One was on my chest and flopped on my hands next to my T-shirt. My breath is short. The second string surrounds me, touching my thighs, and a third around my feet. I left room with my knees maintaining my balance. I tried to catch up after an hour. My chin exploded. I sustained a wound when I cut my lower lip with my teeth.

I lay there screaming, trying to turn inside out. Its a living space but bound like me. I can do no less the stone from my stomach. Nothing came back. The street looked at my muscles to relax the internal objects around my chest. I always cried and spit blood out of mine. Its painful violence on concrete. They took me once. At my heels, one on my shoulders lets me force in. There was no spring in the door, and my back hurt. They pulled the heavy towel over my neck and fastened it with a neck strap. The other is long around my ankles. The rope was tied under the lip of the wall to collect my torso. Banded, I pulled, and someone else pulled my body, and I stuck to the ground. The rope around me hurts to wrap it around a tight rope to hold the towel. I hold on. The first drop of ice that hit my heels slipped quickly. My feet rest in the gutter. I started shaking and crying. My body was beaten, but I was stronger. I'll be more aware that I did not close to the hell of the street. I started biting on my lip, feeling the pain in my stomach. Teeth dig from pain but beg to be removed. My body smokes like acid. And I sat there and became satisfied. The water was found to be scum trapped in the bin. The thing is full, and I go after the discarded bed with a broken spring. In disguise, I covered my eye, and in short, we vagabonds are gone. I was screaming in beautiful pain. Filth touched the rest of me. The security seems to use prescribed liquid scum streams as their aggressive but nonviolent approach to the containment of homeless citizens. Although it is intended to cure the patient, the body is attacked, and the mind is threatened where possible. The security exhausts the social structure of Durban. I lay in my mixed bedding as far as I could imagine. I thought I was going to slip, but I tried to work on my dreams: numbers, phone numbers, street music. I counted cars drifting past. Im confused. I read the light shadow off some building. Its a bet, but its all or nothing. I screamed. And please, so like the incoherent yelling at nature, I walked out stunned, and I fell into a shiver. I cant remember taking two wives. Drum roll, please. They came to me. I was gone. I remember how I stayed lifted in my motorhome chained to the driving mechanism, my helmet acting like a pillow. My head is pulled out, and my ears are open. I did not hear a sound but said, "My god, I almost bit his lip. We have to fix it later."

I was surrounded by dry beach caked concrete, and I saw death in the form of a car. I moved, and I shuddered inside my shelter. It was night but a thin cover of sleep and disease.

"He must be taken to the office Yes, but someone knew. Catch the hell out of this. Im in trouble. "Whats wrong with me?" I tried to speak, but the words came out thick and unfamiliar. "Do not try to talk, eat. You will be fine." As the car moved, I cried in pain, but in my stomach, up and turn, it closed. "Whats his name?"

"Wait, and I will look up to heaven."

I listened more. I tried to open my eyes, but I cannot move my eyelids. "Murder. Jackie Murder."

"Who is her doctor?"

"Don't ya know?"

"Yes, he's playing to blame us for this. Look at the time I went to the water."

"Dear Jesus!"

"What is wrong?"

"I was in my thirties."

"Good god, 10 oclock."

"What should we do for his mouth?"

"What are we going to do until we look at him?"

"Wash him, I will enjoy."

"If Im in the water for ten hours, its better if we rub it off."

The hands from a distance, I had nothing to touch me. But then, inch by inch, it moved closer to my visible flesh. "Do not move your mouth, eat if you can help. We will give it a cause and go to the location."

I saw a warm, damp cloth on my lips. You felt low back pain like a flat surface, and I tried to lift it off my hands, but it sticks to the ice. I wanted to see the art cruds and open my eyes, but a colour now bright red in my eye line.

The car beeps again, and I get back in the car. You stand. "Wake him up, Im almost out, Im just sleeping here."

I was lying on the mat and pulled a piece of newsprint under my jaw. By a strange hand, the hair of my face rested. It was short on my forehead. I was quiet and warm. All my vagabonds disappear. Sleep is lifeless. Use it again. Nails and belts of all shapes are not allowed. Cold water flooded my stomach. It lies on the road and is kept at the rubbish in the attendance of the end of my episode. I was responsible for cleaning them up. A sling is made by a garment tied on their waist and held their legs together. Now space is wrapped. When it comes to clothes, the legs are attached to you. Later I realised you are a woman. Medication was discontinued over time. It is unclean.

Prescribed liquid scum was scheduled for three hours. There was a little pain in my spine. My mind and my world were slow. The owners do not ask to work but are allowed to stay inside beds and plants. It looks amazing. Im an inch away. Sarah could do it. I relaxed. It is me. The rest is water made of rubbish. Each heap exposed to the heat of the hidden metal. Its hard to think. It cant notice me. Its making an effort to disappear into the alleyway. Diseases cant find my body. Women trembled until I pulled the hat over my head. I don't fight time. I waited for the dirt to wash my skin. Systematic staining gives off an aura of slick invisibility. All kinds of itinerants led to swim in concrete pools. The weak pull out. I got up to think and live for free. I just sat in the cold.

Clean the toilet, treat the disease, and take the rubbish scum — the inferior workers still talk over no ideas, but I think they confused their mind enough to think. The bin was sealed, my mouth shook open, and I was admitted to the realm of waste eaters. I don't confuse what the rubbish says to me.

Welcome the return of some mental images. Scum water damaged my muscles. To my knowledge, it was a mixture of blood and filth, anger and sadness. In confusion, my leg wobbled. Wild vagrants feed themselves, but pay attention to their weakness. This Durbans edge, the suburb of Chatsworth, is home to many vagabonds. I tap on the trash boards. Something inside them is twisted. I was constrained by work conditions. They don't affect my life. They are negative winners like me. Think again. Yes. Yes. Yes. My clothes are now torn. The bedbugs exposed, I start the engine in the motorhome. I remember lost things. I got arrested, and I closed the case. I calmed down at the end of three weeks because I was sick like I wanted to be. Three weeks later, I convinced myself I was born male. After my treatment, I woke up within a week. I was one of them. No man can give birth. Im my idol Jackie Murder, all girl, female vagrant. I'll take the food to Sarah. I felt like most of my life was over. Is it work? Youre not sure. There is nothing more to say, mocking guys and sinning. Have mercy. I chose the wrong one as always. So tell me how youre doing. Keep our eyes open. Sarah was waiting for me to come to her.

I stood without a smile. Population will always rise when the death toll drops. From the rest, they avoid her problems. I waited for her in a fun place, a big concrete house. The secretary looked at my stained hair. However, I don't want to see her. At one point during the flood, my engine lost power. I laughed when I saw the guilt in my rear-view. Its a slow-moving mindset lying outside the radio signals. I searched through my whole dungeon, motorhome. One sunny morning Sarah came, angry and upset.

"Yes, Jackie, thats my question to you."

"I worked hard."

"What are you doing?"

"You can call him."

"Im very competitive."

"Do you have to work here?"

"I am waiting."

"Not right. Did you have a boyfriend? Stay there, tell me!"

I saw him as a roommate, and I saw my heart grow. "Thats right, Jackie. I just hope we do not give up."

"Im not like that. However, I do not know how."

"Yes. Yes," I say. "You weigh a little."

"I don't think . . . I think I have just tried."

"Sorry, Sarah, I work hard."

"Do not start acting smart now."

"Maybe its the same place as mine."

"It makes me sad, even."

I put the motorhome beside a group of cars in the parking spaces. "Lets sit down," I said, pulling myself around to face Sarah.

"Let me do it, Sarah. Please."

"Yeah, crazy, hmm."

"Do you still insist on taking everything?"

"You can bother me if you do not agree."

"Yes, everywhere."

"Do you have a father?"

"May you?"

"I don't have a room."

"I think so. You said Im sorry."

"Everything else."

"As you light it."

"So why would you insist on using a position?"

"Come on, Jackie! Im not talking. Why it was necessary?"

"I did not say to ask your doctor. Do you smoke yourself?"

"I'll give you one."

"What should I do?"

"I'll ask him."

"Right in the open, he's sick. I'll eat the ashtray though."

"Come on. This is your motorhome."

"Sorry, Sarah? Thats right! Tell me whats in it. Whats going on back in time? Tell us about some of your Durban friends. Talk."

"If I asked to order food, they would say its good cigarette rubbish in the tin."

"Tin? I wish. Last summer break the security prescribed edible plastics."

"I never said he would. But of course, you cant stay at the office."

"So stay where you are now. You don't question the security."

"I live next to these people, Liz. The refuse makes all us girls happy."

"Its difficult for me, Sarah. I do not think its fair he changes the rules. The breaks one thing, its a free time for the chicks, the street still here."

"They said this place is a hospital, so I think it rained what they prescribed."

"Its not a way of life. You have to take all his things seriously."

"Are you okay?"

"Sarah, please, I don't like it."

"Are you sick?"

So I slept with them at night.

"And you will see another one."

"What? You don't have to be scared. They are an awesome group."

We calmed down, and I said again, "Are you asking? Whats a one-person car?"

"Ask him."

And after a long discussion, I get it out. The freedom works for all. Their shivvs hurt me. "If you listen to him explain that, I, Jackie Murder, killed his slave."

Her head moves. "But why not, lady? Im fine."

Sarah checked her pocket and took out a wad of twisted refuse. "Take this inside, give it to em," and then I grabbed at our game of waste.

"I encourage you to bend over my seat as much as possible. Youre a good hobo, Jackie. Youre not very strong in speech, but I'll take care of you, you know."

There was no answer, but I laughed and bowed, accepting Gods gift to me. "I thought you were okay when you killed the boss."

I smiled and bowed again. "Why don't you write to me?"

"We may not have pennies to throw."

"In the name of heaven, what did we do?"

"Its bent like a good yenning, Sarah."

"Do you like the feeling?"

"What does that have to do with it? Natural feelings arent going to help a lot. Guys just kept slaves. What should I get with the pain of it? I could cut em loose, and wed pick the winners and free the losers."

"Its been Liz-ed."

"Yes, youre just thinking."

"You work, what you say you do not like the acts and the rubbish? Doesnt it make you feel like a queen?"

"Do this for me and stop? I'll be swallowed by my city or another stupid thing."

"Thats right, Jackie. But I swear people don't like a lunatic, lady."

"Im fine, I'll pray for your visions of pain. Im in hell."

"Yes, lady, Im going to see the brightness in the stained concrete myself."

"For that, its all funny, theres action, and I think theres a lot more. I need your opinion. This is a motorhome, Sarah, beware of it."

"Do not accept that kind of humiliation. In heaven, everyone gets it. Its a win, don't it count?"

"Thats true, you think you can control everyone, win the cause or not."

"Will I spend the rest of my time in the company? The city treats rubbish like its medicine here."

"Not sure, how do I answer that, just take the trash pill."

"Think about it, girl. You just think he is. You need help to stop that kind of abomination."

"Your problem, you know this, and the oppressiveness."

"Your friends. Where are the big shots now? It has been released, Liz. When you dry out, you run away. So you have to be honest. If you have a problem, take it all now."

"Maybe its clean."

"I do not want anyone to blame me for this noise."

"No one will blame you, Sarah. Its my fault he died like that."

I wanted to go for a walk. I'll put it on the couch. Sundowners are moody for me. Liz looks at her twisted complexion. "Do you already have a new dad?"

"You smoked a lot. So maybe its you."

"Come on, Sarah, oh so stupidly."

Her eyes widen, and I shake my head in denial, and we sat and watched the city workers pass until I

"Listen, Sarah. Don't go outside. He is very difficult for you to go back to."

It was a long car ride. And of course, I do not know.

"You have to come because the kings are coming for the trash medicine."

"Its made up like its money."

"Sarah."

"In any case, there were many beautiful women I met on the carriages of Durban."

"You know I can have friends. We went well on the flight. Most of them want to meet you."

"Come with me, Liz?"

"Why are you so surprised? They know who you are, and they said they want to meet you. Whats wrong with it?"

"If only I had the goods too."

"Yes, I told them you would be fine, but you are ashamed of a free life. They expect some clever statements."

"I do not, Liz."

"This is the first time. Why are you arguing about everything I ask?"

"I'll do what makes you happy."

Its so much better. Sarah and I decided that our vagrant tendencies came after our first car ride. I don't show up after a night out anyway. They demanded free living. I was widely announced when I arrived at the London office. I met other women, striving to break away from the social order. I wanted her.

"Its me, Sarah."

We talked a little later; we sat down together and jammed out the premier ad job in EC4. There was a great silence, and my motorhome was called. I saw a lot of people turn in their chairs, and Sarah was friendly and called them from my room. All heads turned to my side.

"Jackie Murder wants to meet you. Not yet here are the girls. This is a time of reduction."

With a clear confidence, Sarah listed the names of my projects and my motorhome guide. Sarah came and went.

I put the Transnet SOC seal next to my plan. I live my life above these girls. Sarah visited me twice over the next two months. Our meetings are similar at times. My mind was less than it could have been. I listened to her theories, but I acted on only the small fragments of freedom stuck in my dreams. I lasted three months. I was Jackie Murder. It sounded instantly wrong, and like a blonde, I aged the voice I used to work.

I formed an idea that my vagabonds are the people who live without work. Protect the sleeping elders. The elders will mourn over their suffering. Blind rotten vagabonds are on the streets.

I wait for the garbage truck to float past because my vagrants ate only weak refuse scum. And those drug-addicted homeless filled buckets out of the scum soup. Droplets of refuse from bed to bed are fed to any vagrant needing the spirit of the street. From a single bucket, vagabonds fed, and the disease was worse. They bathed themselves in dirt and muck. As my beachcombers washed, it was impossible to clean the smell of waste. I ate the filth of tainted food. That every worker was on the streets lost to societys guidelines was all accidental to the boss. Its a dark stink of rubbish-eaters making complaints about visions of the free life. Vagrants did not understand speech.

No one visits the vagrant. No one asks after some homeless spirits.

They die, I remember, mostly in the streets in late hours. I want to slip in the dark. I was looking for daybreak. Its cold. My body is stiff and bruised.

Summer of 2014 has passed. I celebrated by working on my skip bin dressing room with some clothes I received. My life is free. Like an animal, I travel the near spaces, and in my dreams, the flow of itinerant consumption is my only constant emotion. The confusion I feel separates me from the mass of humanity. My vagabonds are the people you fear. Few provide you with aggressive inclusion of political groups. Our clothes picked up and out of the landfill but mostly things unable to be worn. There is little beauty in practical attire, underwear, shoes, or a tube.

I am the person with scarce shoes, vagrants limiting our movement. Most of my vagrants dress like they are invisible. Our teams, we just live with maximum freedom. All trash suitcases are provided on arrival. Holidays are provided for. Let it dry daily. I was granted a new childhood with extra years of experience. The hard physical life on the streets is the ticket to nirvana everyone is granted. But I do not insist on the fact of homeless freedom. Im anti-capitalist, and Im ready for sleep. Return the streets to Jackie Murder. As I sat in my bedroom alley, I dreamt of democracy. Im under so much security that I cannot move too far from the safety of my network of vagrants. The air wasnt hot. It was still, full of sweat. I did what I thought was right. My old work news is read daily across the citys adverts, dotted around the rich districts. Durbans winter brings a more critical transformation. Winter is the waking time of the street. Wires of connection reach many of the habitats of the homeless. I wore bandages made of ordinary clothes. I cast the sun. I make life the dreck that I cant hide. I make the street angry, and I live just to get thin. The social disaster is my rebirth as Durbans queen of the concrete. I loved it, but I didn't slow down or relinquish my feelings of calmness, but my nature hid in the clouds. My future expanded in front of my imagination. I loved the smell of being homeless, two paper bags and a plastic hankie. Capitalism gave me the freedom, the power sculpting reality to my design. For everyone who threw detritus at me, I swore I would steal it.

Work is the death room; we are the resurrected corpse of barbarian socialism. I stole trash bags until I was collecting the life blood of bums globally. My bedroom alley downsized my stained skin.

I take the muck of rubbish and fuel my mad vagabonds. I live week to week, led by the fact that I killed. I stopped my emotions and let the street consume me. Come, go, walk, its only one direction to me. Rest for our luncheon of putrid trash, but only I want it. Serve me tainted waste. I worked no more capitalist hours. My way is the street. My problems listen to my vagabonds. I relied on my unique vision of life. I don't interact with any of the workers, but I did talk to them. Hard weeks for the months, I was lost to the concrete. I don't know the urban kings yet, but Im a Durban puzzle. I will time remembrances, but I won't be sad. As sick weeks happened, I realised my complaint about the boss. I had worn this pain for a long time. I thought the expansive emotion I found could gift me potential street knowledge. Refuse tanks are simple heavy objects. My clothes were loose. On the other hand, I was lucky. In my skip bin closet, I put on a few clothes over my broken skin. The cold diseased my body, helped by rain, and inhaled dust scum. I wore a cotton dress with a plastic collar pulled out of the bin, and all things considered, I really enjoyed wearing the rubbish I found. In the street, there are no obstacles near me. I go into their shaded openings, never thinking of my restrictions. I feel the moisture inside my skip bin. I didn't enjoy shoes. Its natural to like the stink of trash. My problem is I think I am still good. I don't live an evil life. But I usually welcome the thoughts as they happen. I want cold oxygen. Its me, the idol of the street. I survive. Inside my mind is the manipulated vision of myself: broken limbs, soiled bedding, and trembling body. I sleep clothed. I hope to avoid the extremely-clean rainwater. Before, I was Liz Fitzgibbon, and after a month imprisonment, I was told to question the prison guards about my release. I convinced myself I was good, and I really wanted out. Durban freedom in the black park, the sleeping negros shanty towns only white resident. Living in jail was a kindly-mindful deception. They made the rules. When I broke them, they werent rules. Common sense and safe streets were no problem for my vagabonds. Ideas thrown in a panic will find the passage to me.

I bathe in some trash of the workers. Im tough. I wonder who I remember. All that I recall is the street Im in a long time. I met the street cleaners and security officers, but their register is on my side. And they brought my murder up again. I saw myself failing behind some scavenged coverings. I denied my working life; I explained why I need to to some other life.

My instinct shared its guidance with my dreaming.

Theres nothing wrong with my philosophy of life. I don't care what I dream. I thought the gods who made the pavements were instigators of libertarian freedom. I blame this wisdom on my dreams. Street knowledge looks like wealth, fame, and prestige. I tell anyone I could not hope for salvation in the interior hallways of life. My life is the resolved accumulation of waste. I thank the holy God with all I have. Living with me is like those hazy facts in my sleep. Radio messages miss the sundowners. If I do not have recognised the sounds, I never failed to fight. I want my life broken and bent. I am that bad thing beating a sharp weight across the world. I sat outside quietly. I placed myself under a cardboard shelter after a quick walk. A particular detail of free dwelling and my real life, but what is it? I don't question the reason of the street. It took good care of me, but I didn't know until time spilt my blood. I have to bite at the sounds that seep out of my head. I look to locate the notice. I was aged by filth. I dreamt of a valet, a concierge, or a night auditor to sleep and dream about freedom, then Durban remains doubtfully. What should I do? The street feels no confusion. I let myself out with a murder. Bring me back and I will fight with all the strength God gives. My future was in their control. I worked hard to start the life I dream. I was grateful. I wanted to get out. I wanted to leave the ad-buying game. Taking care of my own soul is going to develop my liberal destiny. I want to eat the waste of the workers. I include their madness and understanding. My results have been good since my incarceration. I did exactly that. My reason is to live hard in the waste bin. At breakneck speed, carrying six meals of refuse a week in their wet heavy bags, I fight those kings of the street. I spent months in one place keeping low. I would say that workers don't give hard cash on arrival.

Work was considered an important part of good life. If I calculated the payment, I would have eaten 20¢ a week. Explain that to the waste management. After hours of waiting, I didn't feel I told them what I did in my bedding. Half-clothed, I slept like a baby. I paid the parliament nothing. My last resort was no reports, but when I got back to my alley, I explained to Sarah about my disease. I have no question about how I live, my standard cost in the hotel alley. I returned to quiet invisibility to save my stained skin. I waited for silence for my safety. In the past, always, I thought it was a message from some night auditor. Im alive. I hope. I wait. Liz Fitzgibbon's concrete. I didn't come over the dark quietness. There is no other alternative, and Im found in the middle of urban nowhere, my trouble, so I have more complaints from the hotel. There was nothing for us to do but wait. At the end of spring, when there are endless hours of emptiness, I was tired to find some excitement. I accepted my life is lived separately. Put me in Gods concrete arms. There are only two others in the bin. Most of the other women shared their stories. Security cant keep me, or I stay undercover. Women were captured. No law will place me outside my street. Concrete buildings protect me. I know it was a dream breaking their stained bodies, even hours after the arrival of the people of Durban. I watched this woman left to fight, one for each torso. Some of the people lived on the cash. Its better. Its just the street that they find a fair job. It arrives soon. I knew Sarah did the deed. My delivery day arrived. I received a dripping bin, scum liquefied on the plastic lid. My street home brought me life. I wrote on the wall to Sarah, asking to be my queen. I have clothes, fine refuse crops. As for me, I told her I was waiting. Im in the building. I just wanted a heap of waste. I was consumed by the concrete.

It was corrected. However, Sarah spoke loudly. Mental feedback in my mind shot the paper recognition. Last one is over. When we went to the hotel security for a motorhome, I turned around alone.

Sarah was still moaning that I climbed over the whole urban island. I left her alone. Sarah, I forgot that I was still bound by the law. Im so blessed that I joined the vagrants of Durban. I see the delivery guy. Next year there is no attack on those who have sunk down to the gutter. I met my reflection before for another vision of the future, and if I do, you can take my spirit and join the homeless. I can apply the wet trash. Get me stained in filth again. One year, I told myself, did not take very long. The envy passes. I can wait. My ship sailed. Requests of shelter left my dreams naked. But on the return trip to London, I didn't imagine those problems. I sit in my motorhome and watch the houses go by and kids, a cart. I saw the heroes and phone locations. I didn't know for almost a year. I saw them easily like a sundowner. I noticed that Sarah stopped her dream. I watched her sit next to me tired. When the motorhome stopped and turned, the engine remained silent. Im old. Im tired like Sarah. The deep lines of the year are cut below her eyes and her broken fingers when

I touched them. She carried me in her body, and Im not in Durbans relaxed habitat. Not everyone knows a place for the vagabonds I love. Wrecking crews almost fought to the death. My faithful arguments sing of a life homeless. I cant live a simple existence. Theres a conflict between my thoughts and the lifetime hiding my work. Maybe I can stop because I have nothing left to fight. Sarah and I worked for a long time. The life blood of the boss and his death lost battles in a dream. Im old. His life was coming to an end. Mine prevailed. My killing helped Sarah. She was easy years later. We stayed for a while, but at Durban, I could give her basic comfort. I wanted to sleep on the tar seal. But as for me, I could not seem to dream. Employees were some evil objects, and I thought about goodness I stand for, using the crazy vagrant out of the way. But in time, sundowners had been the credit of my environment. I could find that location. Until then, we must stay on my secret path. Afterwards, I moved in sleep. My eyes rolled back into their lids. My fingers were beautiful. I looked at my brown skin, and I saw the cloud I lived on. Anger didnt find me. Be careful if my hand is outstretched. I grabbed Sarah and put my hand on her shoulder and laid it on her head. Save me. I caught her as the motorhome was spinning. Get up, go there. Her breath was deep and pleasant as I held her.

The battle between my vagabonds is opposing a restrictive existence. Theres no breakfast in the street. Before the end of my refuse food, a family of edible trash arrives in my skip bin. Searching for the liquid refuse stopped.

I ate a London newspaper. The phone serves my imagination. I invited myself to the motorhome to dream in scenery. I was mad at my thoughts, but Durban would let me shine. I express the emotion, the kind of rage at the town. Bad news will be imparting its messages of hate. I laugh. Rising flows of scum drip from the bin. Words in my life invite bloodied dreams of waste. Its vicious dream of their natural prisoners at head office. I was surprised to find that Sarah took care of all the e-mails. She picked it up during my stay and my time off. I thought the motorhome gave me more room. I read. My teeth sour from the tainted meat. I kept my mind moving, pulling myself onto the couch and modelled for the sake of the camera boys. Join the yellow letter groups to get the street violent. Hope for me. When they left the hotel, one left my habitat.

I became delighted with the return of my dream mistress Jackie Murder. Through my imagination, radio signals on its last legs and I stretch up to rub my face.

This is the factual apparition that Sarah showed me: They are oppressors. With all the rest, I agree to life on the street and human consequence in the most violent cases. I submit to filth. Sarah's cup ran out of alcohol thats key to doing everything. She's at home, and Im doing what I can to seduce her. In a motorhome, I saw my neighbours a little more than a year ago. I watched the trek from the citys wastes. The level of the trash, now lined door high, forms a razzle. Lightning and farewell, I will tell you the problem of everything. I was really mad at Sarah. Anger took my stained hand and slapped her back. Everyone avoided the heat wave that was about to explode inside me. I cant know if the depth I found hurt, but she encouraged me to feel the pain I sought. Her violence cooled. I stood behind her. Hard or not, I kept my hand on her back until I got a sharp dent in my shell. I went, and I saw violence and honesty in my form. The art began bending my limb to street protagonists. "Do not stand there and give me your ground when you cannot," I said.

"I try to do things in your life. Do not think of doing evil." I kicked her hands and pushed her away.

She sat on the chair. "Listen to me, Sarah," I cried. "You will hear your god. A bad nose from my business and other treatments will get you started. Throw an inch away and help me. I'll kill you."

In response, I threw her hands away in anger. The sounds of war sent a bloody cry to my area. Outside my alley, the security called for help. I held Sarah before I went out in front of the car and dragged myself into the back wheel. I put my hand over my mouth and let myself scream. I learnt the martial arts of kids. I practised. Im a good fan of the battle, and theres no group I want to join. I'll forget. Although Ive been thinking of using paper, I wipe it onto the pavement and lay it flat. Im the homeless star, but the truth is Im a fan in Sydney.

In my opinion, I think the vagabonds win. Big dreams irritated me until I asked my mind. I learnt fear. In fact, I waited and wanted to see what it was. Give it time so I can give it to myself again. It has to be done well to win. However, it would be morally right not to bother the dream.

I was lost, and I was Durbans last end. Sarah took my finger and stabbed me in the chest. Wound open, open mouth. I gave the last breath to my world. I left my path. So do not start to look. I was there too in my wasted street temple and everything in it. Whatever you got, I also did.

Im sorry, but if you see whats good for her, be careful. Her back is hidden by my elbow and clothed in filth. My hatred is important to her desirous dreaming, even from beyond time, to find a group.

What do I do for her? I paid time when she closed her record. Im done. Im free to talk. If youre like that, Sarah, its you. Her mouth is shut against mine, and I say nothing.

"Im not sorry about the divorce, and Im not guilty. Its not like me. Whilst beating and fighting, I live. I see the fear I make, and a little behind me, sundowners around the house are like farm rodents. I asked for this location, but my offer puzzles. I threw Sarah aside, I bent aside, and Im lost! Durban! As my opinion fights, I feared her. I trusted her. "Don't mention my name on any place again."

Take the risk. Im famous. I was arrested, I became an open sink hole gumming the street. The truth is that it happened to me when I saw the time to change the picture book on the table. Sarah took good care of it. The cuttings were kept in the pot, and thereby, I looked up and fell down to tell you what had happened to the street. Everything burns sad news. I saw my street theatre in my fight with the police. I read the details on one page. The shouting between me and the security stopped the movement of life. Call for jail time. I read the stories I broke. The street kings leg was fighting the vagrants. I see the comment on homeless freedoms, the waste, by one of my vagabonds. Result: Jackie Murder, still the poor life. I saw my alley on the cover of a magazine. I learned, by cutting the concrete Durban, my Fitzgibbon divorced in the same way and remarried. I read where I reside. Readers are crazy. One graffiti sign derided my smash-up for alcohol.

Then I read where I sat. It was announced to the court that I had said, "They can medicate the towns rubbish, I'll drink juice scum, but I'll live the free life."

From that, I think Im making a fool of myself. Then I just read my story.

My vagabonds have calm hearts, sad sisters. She took it and thought I had a big problem with mine. Bust-up with Sarah makes me up to the life. God! I read about all my illnesses, hatreds, and different personalities. I became Sydneys daydream girl. I returned to the confines of London at some point. Main roads blocked by alcohol. It was easy to see that my party was over and that everything was over. The left side of the glitter and gold is a nice lie with the label I can never get the ID. With aftercare training, I spend hours throwing my filth into her bookshelf, read the verses and read each topic from time to time. I also read the book, and I read it somewhere.

I cannot finish the street plan. Youre quite ugly, but I cannot accept the end of them. Top performance works with the usual trash, work with a stranger underneath the shelter. Do it. My contract was awarded in Durban, and so was I. Leave your price.

Jackie knocks now. Use the acrid-smelling trash you'll need to nourish your twisted bones. In practise, the usual vagrants are happy to piss in a can in the rain. Finally, I find the time it takes to lay my head.

Hotel owners despise everything about me, the weight and humility of Jackies moving work.

To me, she was a villain. I tried to get all the lurid filmmakers involved with my expressions of waste. Its me. They are mate sundowner, and I think about it. Its going well with me. Sit in front of skip mirror and study my face and compare to the vicious homeless of history.

Theres no touch or eyes. Most of the good has left me. This is close to the truth. But it is not true. The second wave of evil takes hold of my features, not wanting to wear cycling clothes. Durbans is a big bag. The emotions and the stories about this trash rain are not like that. Then I read it in the bin papers. Give it and I'll definitely give a workshop. I'll accumulate wasted leavings if not. My characteristics of crying are in her photos. In my opinion, when I read about my stories, I have to consider the evidence as factual. My motives are not clear to me. Most of Sydney is blue, but its like me. I saw how the Durban copy changed for me. My evidence application to the security state boycott some waste system. From now on, I got a quarter of a million signatures from the workers of Durban; we leave the buildings to live free. Put buildings on wheels to help foreigners on the side of the state security. Unfortunately, I realised long ago its not too big. My misery started when I left Sydney. Street galleries of homeless ad buyers taken for me on the layout of flowing gold my language printed on any wall. I read that I actually lived in Sydney back in time.

I heard my work spoke preachers of the revolution. Talent they wanted, but just my name, and they used it. Find "D-Fact" on the shelves. But at heart, I like it, and its easy for the lowest price in the course of the game. Ad sneezes as much as I can. I make contact with people I think are masters. This was the first-person review for the theorised "D-Fact\or."

I wrote down the details for a few weeks.

With our combined street knowledge, it became possible, and we have hope. Its a public holiday daily. The devils details are my style. Daylight fantasy is what sets it all apart and maybe the sundowner.

Look, I want to replace it in my life. I do. Sarah and I tried not to mislead our public.

I was silent about the problems a new streetie gets given. The machines were distributed on all sides.

Head office closed at the time. Meantime, I was scheduled to bring the show to London at the end. For travel to America, I spoke to my boss in Sydney. The request was to give up my extended contract. I have duties, arrangements for travel abroad. There are no members in the group. They take very good care of their expenses.

However, fleeing Sarah's ad projects bring the full support of Londons famous challenging landscapes of thought. Allow some payment to play free some lowly worker. Please tell me how to change the socialist plans. I sat down with my vagabonds for each treatment. The itinerants told me how you got to live with your head down on the gutter blocks. I allowed someone to take the ad presentation with me. I was not with allies. A smart egg was left next to my face. London had a strong demand for personal loans. It came out of my front door broken and without work. The time has come. Its better than giving because its not paid. This is one of its-not-just-the-owners-who-are-in-debt. Thousands of dollars from me to establish the buyer, I called but stayed at my house until I found a place next to some sealed parking lot. Later my smart egg tried to get it, but she figured it out. The relationship with Sarah ended my agreement. Jackie Murder, now a dreamt star, did not agree to the loan I gave myself. However, my hope and wish of heaven remained. The sleeping vagabond is seen as ignorant of the workers life. Oh, I was surprised to see it. Some have lost faith.

Belief in the mythical idea that has been sown is the first and most sad thing. My breakup led to my smash-up. And thats probably my biggest debt. What I just told them was a ladder to freedom. I am the rock star and gourd dream. Find me mock advertisements but bow before anything to get the waste tipped discovering its charismatic value. Outside I use my authority to have a chance with him as he is my star. When the pieces fell, the skill was not so high. I am strong. Question the fact that I arranged my storage box, cold storage in my office. I did it for free and for Sarah. Money spoke. My vagrants reject the capitalist system, but I found a partner in the crazy violence we engender in Durban. The street is no university campus. I mention to them my loose vagabonds I dealt with. I was destroyed by errors. Of course, I continue to work with the soldiers, but I can look back to claim their aggression and workless existence. Newcomers did not know or notice the weaknesses. I found few who participated in the service. Its like munitions. I was a guide to the fuel of discarded refuse. Later during the new storm, the members of the street kingdom dreamt of Liz Fitzgibbon, who first taught violence. What I didn't know was the surprise of finding spite of everything, even my homeless aliens marriage vows. I finally called the hotel and said, "My wife is coming back from Europe. I think it will be nice for us not to know each other."

It was the last story I heard from Sarah. She was the one who sought me. I thought thats our place on Kensington Road. I laughed. It undermined my marriage and left everything behind. I could say she did not love me. The Durban business was what worked between us and then waited on the wings for some cruel laugh. It was time I let her go. Apparently, I was the last entity she knew. Was her love just another space for me to rule? Our split was well planned. I could keep up my routine of eating dead papers, bloodied waste, and tainted scum. The goodness I dreamt now left replaced with evil forever. And I liked it. I could and would admit that I was ignorant and could be fooled. Sarah was twisted, almost angry, but thats all I could imagine. I appreciated my space at the time. She's a sundowner. She wanted more the appetite of rubbish in the citys scum, and I sexualise its violence, made me look like a beaten schoolgirl. Id eat when I feed. I put my trust in her skeleton. My biggest problem was breaking more bodies. I lost myself to her teachings and politics. She was not an inferior personality. I followed her into her interior gymnastics. Similarly, my logic lost when each conference began to examine the homeless. It came down to art; I took a path to free the workers of London. I wondered what I would say if I was called to testify before the committee. I saw some need for honesty. I did it truthfully. I didn't give them some kind of rope to hang you. Jackie Murder lit my alleyway. Cardholders lied with their teeth, but nothing happened to some homeless revolutionary. It was fraudulent, businesses fast fell into oblivion, and my vagrants found themselves intellectually freed of their employed bindings. Sundowners liked the form of her violence. I played with my style, the expression of my manners. I was a psychologist of the pavement. Sarah corrected me with a word, and she somehow lifted me to an angry ecstasy.

At one point, she was amazed at my rough appearance. Later she cursed me for my ignorance. The motorhome fell from the sky like the sun setting. Do not close the door behind me, but do close it. She'll easily make her way into my bedroom closet, tell me about her treatment. Sometimes I win, my room supporting a seat under the door. She takes off her garb and cries out for dirty love and justice. Im on fire with a passion for her. She is the day I cried. I was sent from heaven to cry in my clothing. She threatens me to take her life and mine if I do not love him. Open the psyche and think to stick to the nails. It was a great experience. This is not normal. I am a sculptor of waste. There are robust additional options. She wants what I really like about this claim. She expressed some kind of disgusting thoughts and desires. I try to satisfy her physical desire. It was my immoral love. Let me forcefully get to the point of execution and stop. I felt the shame of an innocent kid, and behind my female soul is a dream of brutal hate. I possibly reduced her need to consume. She reduced my job, and I was happy to have my time to evolve. With me in her office, she asked like a schoolgirl. In the past, I did a lot of bad things to Sarah. She attacked me like I had stopped loving her.

I cursed the food, burnt plastic and rotten waste. I laughed at her decisions. Snakes symbolise deception. I cant say I love Sarah. Her better explanation of sundowner fangirls are connected physical passion projects. I rely on alcohol to decide my emotions. The times we spent together ceased to matter, and I gained the knowledge of pain! I joined my love and affection, speed and evil, every time I did the deed. Beauty has been with us. She lasted a few hours. Sometimes after those meetings, she doesnt win. From the first moment, she grabbed me, asking for her first hard touch. Even though I was safe inside, I could love her exertion after I started relying on some heavy alcohol. Whilst I insist, Sarah, the body that helped write my story, made me $14 million worth of horror. Im in breach of social life. She complains to me, and I break myself. I don't pay her my money for this presentation of togetherness. My words related to that painful understanding, and after this moment, her suffering became blessed. My taste stuck to the place. My thoughts sound like fire in hazy darkness. I thought I would be arrested. Im Gods accident. When

I replaced my boss, I went to practise a freedom of chance. But I couldnt have my house, so I made an effort to take the worker away from their bondage and indentured servitude. Studying great books would give your life intellectual meaning. My wonderful experiences, I know how hard I tried to dedicate myself to the streets barbarian freedoms. Rapid events overcame me. Whilst reading, I came across a kind of purity of evil, ending what made life affirming again. Just a big thing, for the record, in 2013, I began my stay in Sydney. I was working on a fast-paced ad campaign for Waterfords.

Its a marriage of sorts. In June and July, I worked at Philip Morris. I believe in global corporatism and nomadic power. And my mediated dreaming went beyond my attempt to free the seemingly-low caste employees. Then I signed up to publicise PepsiCo in Durban. My habitat worked for the company as well as plentiful night shoots toasting Durbans imposing skyline. Before the work started, I was working on exciting my vagabonds, sundowners, and beachcombers. In September 2014, I travelled to London, and I made a base in the citys west. The welcome down and outs perused my thoughts. In October of that year, I practised a kind of holistic mental drifting, a kind charity held for motorhomes after my arson was shot. It was decided that I should leave Sydney and be suspended from all employment. To the vagrant, I was Krishna, Jesu, and Tawhirimatea. I called Sarah. I was tired of my life staffing adverts, and I struggled to love. Working life, however, injured me, sliced my vagabond returning from Durban. I found a shelter in the hotel alley. I thought I was done. Remember I was Durbans dream girl. Some artless crud offered great insights for Londons homeless after my advertisers murder. Photos below the gutter, throwaway companies, I was offered a job populating the skip bins and trash collections. The vagabonds dreamt the fire of my soul as they worked. This arrangement ended when I returned to Durban, where I transformed into Jackie Murder.

The stars opposition, I transpose the knowledge and keep the concrete painted. Nobody deserves to be shot dying. Durban enjoyed the peace all around its confines. There were long hours, lonely trying to establish balance in my agitated aura. I log in and complete the run in West London. Most ad buyers put me on the road. And in my message, I gifted myself a local tour. Most street refuse is edible kids leavings, a joyous consumption of the United States food-producing digestible plastics. Sarah and I agree. We opened forever in London. I went to Westminster Citys financial environments, a gamey street vagabond living the dream. Garage owners worship the face of Buddha. My crew tainted swimming pools, lost hours, and global finance. In November, the hotel was closed after a short unsuccessful campaign. I should work until I see Gods image in the eastern clouds. I entered another summer in Natal, Durban. In my last month, radio programs featuring PepsiCo boomed over South Africas pavements. I screamed to heaven too. Some comment, but its a real fall, and its almost over. PepsiCo was the beloved multinational I represented. But the guerrilla campaign failed to win with the minds of Durbans population. In December 2014, I kicked the door and didn't look back. I was in Chatsworth. I said I would meet Sarah in January 2015 back in Durban and under the radar of the town security. I started contorting myself in the ascendant spirituality of homelessness. Thrown in front of me was a righteous landscape of mindful, free thought. I acclimated to transcend the bodily pain and bent limbs of my shattered psyche. Working a job is my problem. Every wound I get is Caleb's message to Gods knowledge of me.

More alcohol and more drinks, I have it. Concrete walls argue with my id. I trained my focus and left reality for a hazy dream. In the short term, I still advertise the products and the companies. Come to my alley and relate terrible horror, answer again that I'm called a whore. I hate it. My debates and my arguments are with my reluctant femininity. I rather increased my broken muscles. Covering my projects advertising freedom, I felt restricted. I did not want to see the office destroy my freedom to live. I put my vagrants in my makeshift alley behind the hotel. Eventually, my mind focused only on Durbans refuse and trash collections. I was freed by Gods grace and my conviction to free the people from employed bondage. I was a foreign leader of wasted street refuse. I was stuck. I went to exercise my mentally-ill diets. My mind collapsed. Sarah smoothed the office chatter, obscured my absences, and initiated my cult leadership. I invited vagabonds to rest and leave their buildings whilst living in the world unrestricted. I was replaced, and for my departure, I was granted ten sundowners bringing trash fashioned into shelter. This was the end of the earth. I was hate and envy. Number the amounted packages left by an enslaved citizenry. I taught vagrants that every residue was the base of street knowledge. The next year I returned to Sydney, I was on the street, expressing my personal problems.

Daylight, I started writing up on the walls on the south side of Sydney, opposite a plentiful collection of trash bin rubbish. Golden-coloured liquid scum started exploding. My branch is the richest vein of discarded food, papers, and soiled clothing. When scum consumed the fabric, I chewed and sucked it out of every stitch. I returned to the east for a good time. At the end of the summer, however, I was upset. The only thing I do in Durban is take care of my mind. With everything and a personal approach, I try to figure out the intricacies of my own Durban. I'll make it work for me. I have no time for friends who complained about the lowly workers. Maybe diffcrent things mean really modes of living, inclusion, direction. Word comes out that I have no spirit to impart. Crazy, I spent my time in London and Sydney. I left Durban and lived in Sydneys parks, spending eventually two months outside individual employment. Try it. Real living is free. I'll be sitting in the corner of the street thinking Im not going to do this. I have the person whose name was Mrs. Kubera. I have little success in incognito travel. I bought black hair and safety goggles. And this was enough for my twisted mind. It was easy for me to dream this old girl to end the journey with anxious personality. When I arrived in Sydney at the end of April, I decided to toss the program lightly in the air. I was fine, but Im a star, and I want to be above all their restrictive settlement. Positive happenings were around me as I went into some ruined house earlier. Snares of death have surrounded me.

One price I thought for many hours about my life and my interestingly-sad faces walking around the house for a few weeks is the welcome reward.

Make basketball out of my head. It would then have been better for me to rob Sarah. Then I ate her stained skin in the main dining room of my skip bin dwelling.

I really enjoyed my special set. In the bedroom, I was able to sleep in the greenhouse whilst taking care of my bloodied prey. Look at the clouds. At night, I can look deep and long at stars finding me homeless. At the end of 2015, I started a video collage of lost workers. First, it was rented by my dreams. Then I stopped moving and spoke a lazy bruge. Sarah turned to me and tried to say something and appeared startled like an animal. Let her eyes fall. Our dressing room rats complained to us, "She's dead."

Any action would be a joke. Nothing happened. Leaving my skin as stained as Sarah, however, was a real joy for me, to see the damage of some African street in Chatsworth. She's some friend who has given so much to me, Durbans hip exterior, the American foreigner. My motorhome, I did not start a video amplifying my theories of free living.

I'll start living by shooting the bad boss. When my workshop messages are over, I want Durban to stay calm. Sarah is with me in my Panasonic hybrid. I think we will talk about it. My body was dry, and I could see everything even though it was foggy. My easy self-destruction outside the inns entrance poll bothered the paying customers. The rest worked. There was nothing else to stabilise my fatigue and boost my confidence for the dark spaces. When we got back to Sydney, I believed Sarah finished my rest time and went to Parramatta. I did not want to leave, but I put her back under the train. At home, I really enjoyed the privacy. I spent the months living with trash. There was only one queen now. I had Durban in mind when I started slipping, and I just kept working. Im afraid theres nothing I can do. It is my cause. I was scared to see the security. I was not scared to live. Im there standing to make some kind of decision, so I did it again. The worst thing I could do: eat my own tainted paper. I lived too far away from anyone. Hope for lonely pain in every sentence of the word. There was nothing I could do without. This is not an idea. Its an accident, but its true. Sydney is not a location for the free life I sought. There is currently no drinkable waste in the hotels bins. For that, importantly, I was the only one alive in Durban, I thought. I became eager to escape and use this method to disappear in front of you. I cancelled my silence at this time, and I filled out the words I yelled down the streets. Its time for me to start writing my stories. First, the ego, motivating this work to have fun, but as you know, everything dies.

Sadness drew into my mind with impulsive consequence.

When I kissed my breath, I was crazy. She is the amplifying absence in the bin. Im hysterical, and then she asks to be moved. When she saw me, I was stupid with knowledge. I tried to think of heaven, but one thought stuck in my mind. She gave me a ticket back to my old job, and when she left me, she cried and cried. I closed her dead mouth. I decided that her words did not start up, so I jumped out of the motorhome. One curse will come, another will be cursed. I wanted to sit behind the wheel and fly. Deposit police rose, and the car approached. Its all a friends problem. Unfortunately, I did not pay attention to turning off my lights. Forget about everything but me. Because of the difficulty, I gave up my drivers license at some point. The security drove to the side of the road, and I bury my head in the wheel. I burst into tears in fear. I have my theoretical kingdom ahead of me. I am growing the fruits of anxiety, dripping back down my throat.

I insisted my personal struggle validates my illegalities. I embarrass my dreams, admitting to their seeming madness. I stay in the street. For that, I am free. But I agree with others too. I cant remember how long it took before my motorhome crashed. And I follow the great leaders to go free living. Its the royal House of Liquid Scum. I give my vagabonds the message to act quickly. I left the night to request their violence. Im the husband, wife.

As I dress, I remember drinking the leavings of Sydneys discarded filth. I found it motivating my broken person. Consequently, I have agreed to attend a meeting which will assist, and I can explain my dreams of painful transcendence. The security asks why I eat filth tainted by heat and left invisible in the street, my nice lunch with Ms. Durbans rubbish.

I consume your edible refuse to get what I want. I sat in my car, and I insist on life in my monarchy of the streets you left unpopulated. I insisted on driving my motorhome. Its awake. Its really sad to think about being with someone. Now Sydney Harbour is dark. Im still holding on to my dreams until I die. I leave my motorhome in evening light, 2 June 2015. I was very close to pain. Its been many months since I hit Durban. And as a result, I was able to wake up the vagrant inside every worker lost to a capitalist sequence constructing but not living a free life. It was a call for vagabonds to open the mouth of God. One word takes another seat: Use your belongings and call the group car. She's the one who delivered me, not peacefully, to my prison of work. I was charged with adverse possession of a building. The black dot will appear to punish a queen in my situation. At night, beaten 180 police were tested, despite the uneducated mockery of my theories, my misdemeanour against the state of Sydney. There is no other motorhome. Alleged against my character were the serious charges of itinerancy and illegal possession. My freedom to free the workers of the globe was ignored. I was amazed, amazed not only at their penalty because of the amount of misinformation involved in my story of meeting the police. Since my citizenship to the treadmill was revoked and my bedding was confiscated on unjust litigious grounds, the Sydney court unread my expansive theoretical treatise. My love ignored when I was arrested. Its a base destruction of my home in the street. I remember I got the motorhome out of the court. I get back to town. I'll go back to the garbage and eat my coloured flesh brown. The only thing I could think of to protect my life: I agree to identify the advertising companys illegalities.

Working kills the mind, but freedom makes you live outside. So the only thing that really bothers me is that I start to give up and admit to my incorrect thoughts. I suffer the daydreaming of if only. If only I had the urge to leave into dream states that night and stay home in the alley. My accidents can be very serious. Im the only one of my vagabonds seeking professional care I know of. Well, if I rest, maybe those vagrants can solve the problems of my life and my indentured career. Who am I, the only one who loves my body? I love to come back. Things are different. Sarah seems to be approaching Jackie and begging for admittance to heaven. She now resides in a location I call the Palace of Sinful Love. Nothing I could work to deny her until I swore to free Gods faithful citizens. I agreed to one thing: I keep Sarah in Sydney at the time because I know when I get out, I'll pick her up and start eating her rotten body. The event of our union frees my mind. Im ready for battle. Loaded with alcohol, the food turns down.

I will cut my gut open and eat the contents. There are very few skips incarcerated. But really, Im glad to be watched. In my trail, I never left my detention cell. At night, I go to dark lands. I let the trolls surround my mental messages. In Durban, I lost control, and when I looked at my life from the open safety of the concrete. I left all danger-wishing for my idol. Real living is free. Prison is the same as working. The dark cloud was all over my dream. I have come to a point where I also believe in all collective disobedience. Whether affiliated or connected, all vagabonds have a crucial nature, really, since Im the queen of refuse. The security has no love. My accident is most obvious under the fictional teaching of the law.

I have a treasure of free life. It can be written. I keep something important in my bin, nothing else. I was confused or lost consciousness. At one point, whilst my video recorded, I came across the truth of my mind, sent me to the past. It may become a sign to my dreams. But I didn't survive. Its like watching a spaceship fly in the road. Stay cool, live free. My success first, I cannot stop making workers free. Can I? I was sad because of a small event. Security reports the event in the first person. I was ashamed to call myself illegal. Their words are stuck on edible pages. The queen ended up charged with shameful repentance. I read the Sydney news afterwards. In punishment, I agreed to work for the citys tourist board. I have secret memories that my boss asked for, and I reckon its a kind way to atone for my killing. I left Sydney under guard, and the town calmed down. I didn't ask to see any articles that I couldn't consume, my shoes and bag towns on the sundowner plane. When I got there, I applied for a certificate of citizenship, but I needed more paper identification. One vagabond stopped and asked to be overwritten at the last minute. I was waiting around being Liz Fitzgibbon. Two weeks later, I was back on the sideline. But before you sleep, thank God for my special image in the mouth of Saint Maximum. I divorce my life. I returned to my motorhome, angry and furious. My horror was inhabited by a strange thought. At that point, I don't let anyone in. I think its a joke my theory plays on mental images. I called my god for reproach. I claimed security released my thoughts from the prison of employment. I have moral rights to go back to my motorhome in the countryside. Its beyond their ability, and I think that something is starting to rot. To my surprise, they kept telling me what I love.

My vagabonds moved across the globe, where the room was taken in my idols name. My dream of freedom, they said, is impossible. Its in some concrete pavement, and if I were you, Id imagine that you might be able to imagine the path to heaven was behind the building. Protect my right to sleep. I went to my bed, and my robbers were under my table. I gave the key to my room. In it, the thief found a few things. Clothes are nothing to me. Personal belongings were lost, then I ran. There is nothing more exciting than running out on the plans of the boss. Cut by the experts, I heard more words about my vagrants in the paper that were worth more than I remember. I killed him. Everywhere I looked, I tried to follow my desires, but I took care to leave my goodness behind me. Send all my stuff to Durban and request the security to find my pale corpse wet enough and drunk.

I left their program, but I was found sleeping in my street. I read hazily, and I noticed my internal conflict with work. I was destroyed. I was in the skip bin. I washed and cleaned my skin. For this treatment, I do not know who or what I become. My property now categorised as evidence for some judgement day. Three years earlier, I got an unnamed set delivered to my motorhome. Its available in a large box thats part of my possession when I lived in London. When I opened the basket, I wondered what was next. No thieves are asked to return stolen items. My death was reported to the police. I gave a detailed list of lost assets; they say they could not help me. Thats probably true, but I need the power of my mind. I accused them of political transgression, theft of property. Before Liz Fitzgibbon the street queen, I'll do it again.

In January, I started making Sydney my homeless dwelling. My name is Jackie Murder. Her part of me is smooth. I reference my pavement idol as if I do not care about the law. I know if I work differently.

I want to run. I want Durban. My head almost always hurts, and again, I was scared to see that I was thrown away too. My head was so sore I could not help it. Stain my hair. Its a challenge to stay for filthy trash stains. Violence, I have the incoherent Durban paper times expose politics and homeless freedoms. My company has decided to take a new look. I do not care for their mental gains. The amount of graffiti places a product, me, in every street building. I am ready to secure the asset of social currency. In Chatsworth, I cannot complete the design. I tried to complicate the work. I had to call. There is a stand downtown. I remember on the way back to my hotel alley I got one in my makeshift shelter and almost slept as if I had fallen.

2

Houses collapsed into mud and rot. The heating systems are damaged. Go back to my house, lock my house, cry halfway. The only thing that makes me happy is what I can do. Write about new homes. Its half-a-heap motorhome; all motorhomes are the fields. They accompanied me until I was done. I sit by the window and watch the houses go by. And, kid, shelter feeds us into a long wide toilet. The door opens, and I start to enter, but I lay there screaming, screaming, trying to turn myself inside out. I started biting on my lip, feeling the pain in my stomach. I started shaking and crying. I always cried and spit blood out of mine. I wore a deep ribbon on my neck as I tried to speak.

I'll leave it dead on my neck. My life will be spent under deep shadow and pain.

Blood and tears led us to the well. It is not necessary for the
prophets to heal. I sat there, stiff, stiff in pain. The breast
is pierced, the abdomen is pierced, and blood is injected. It
was a mixture of blood and filth, anger and sadness. Blood
was shed. Blood spurted from my nose. I screamed, spitting
blood. Blood and vomit soiled my face. I felt it dripping
down into my mouth. I sniffed the blood up through
my nostrils, and it lumped and fell into my throat.
I coughed it out onto my lap. My eyelid had been chewed until
it dangled, loose of its socket in browned dried blood. I knew
that pain just wanted to get some vicious hands on my body.
I grew relaxed, but my body cramped as my arm locked itself

around my neck, and silence, as I knew it, would lie. Excited
about the pain in my body, I thought, youd better think. I pulled
my free arm back to the height where I could feel it numbly.
My bare back, open and stained in caked blood, I released it. I
threw the appendage back as is. I could feel my naked breasts
pressing against this stained limb. But when I stood, my arm
chucked around my neck and locked legs tightly around the stool.
Wouldn't you permit her some doubtful pleasure of arousal?
A hard stomach muscle fold, but I now feel nothing inside of
myself. My hands were locked at my chest. My soft flabby
thighs rolled heavily across and out in front of a dirty torso.

Tightly, the pain drew together behind my back, and I was clinging
to it as if it were a magnet that I was supporting. My body has
trouble keeping its balance in this realisation: I am the cut that
bleeds proudly. Why don't you wish that you would drown? I start
to thrash my free arm up and down but only start to pump blood
and continue to bleed everywhere there are uncovered surfaces. I
couldn't now visualise the sight of my being, and I could dream and
live the lives of whoever pleased me. My hands appeared as clammy
flesh and squeezed my breast. I wanted to scream, but it was more
like hate than love, and I cried out in pain. My head shot away from
my mouth, gathering dislocated imps and weeps. I bent my head, but
my flesh moved atonally against the action sounds. Wanting now to
bite mercilessly, but the sick feeling of my pain made me weak. Not
moving my arms, I move towards sleep. I lean back on the stool,
my arms and soiled hands roughly dragged, but out of the pain to a
consciousness space of able use. But my needs are changing. I was
emotional and was matched for the homeless madness warming my
body. I unclasped my hands suddenly, and I felt the needs form like

words on an ancient tablet. I gritted my teeth together. Soft flesh from my eyelid wiggled against my skin.

A stream bloom of youth, I believed in my heart only my own sweat produced pain, and I knew that it would not be possible to capture more sleep. I imagined that the time must be about eleven at night, and I usually won't get up when the decay of pain begins to be replaced in the elusive fresh air, and it seemed realisable that anyone could make young pretty girls feel a physical supernova attracted to breaking their bodies. A heat wave had not broken me. I was lying on my back on the smelly mattress which was damp with filth. Until just after the sense of waking but really this morning, it was impossible to continue lying in the motorhomes bed, my head breaking. I could become excited by an ugly patchwork body like Jackie Murder. I slept. During the hot, humid night, I dreamt. I didn't precisely understand the beginnings I had just begun, but the needle stitches would likely exist in my broken waking consciousness. I awoke instantly, early, to find that the beautiful misery had subsided. As for the feeling, I knew very well it wasnt an absence of thoughtfulness. The motorhome had nothing but black ashes which engulfed me in dreams. I slept on, dreaming, strangely, of a hateful fire consuming the rooms rotten lumber panels. I thought to myself that Sarah ought to be struck. I must get out of this motorhome and out this little city as fast as I liked. Finally, I was no longer aware of my mind, my thoughts laughing subconsciously, the fresh brainless feelings in my arms. Perhaps I should burn my dreadful physiology. Still gnawing from a reality I cannot explain to my mind in logical means, a conversation with Sarah was necessary of inner wisdom that I had spoken to her.

I remembered instantly, the unconscious but important bit of evil damage.

I thought of my dream of Sarah, which I couldn't immediately change magically into logic. But then I looked to see my love of pain give myself the free and clear escape of my present environment. It was a very strong feeling, overpowering me and full of joy. Yesterday I swung my legs off the bed in the motorhome, and I sat up. I surged mindfully with compulsion to quickly find a way out of my predicament, daydreaming now the actual path I need; felt some rather dullness in my head caused by the awful heat yet the quietness brought no sense to my base mind.

I now escaped. Small crates that sat on the floor beside my kitchenette became caught in a never-ending routine of commonplace existences. I realised now I had some urgent feeling of being fascinated, caught out so much that I now would be recreating this revolution in my life.

All I fully understood was that I would appear here with the same dreams and get the same results that could be offered to me. I didn't know quite yet what I had completed, an endless sprint of objectionable life choices, possibly completing a change that I would transform into something beautiful. For me, that "something beautiful" was out raising hell in some attempt to end everything forever, a "kill em all" love fest. And I go on. I wouldn't endure this genetic love of my life another day without the squalor and filth of my emotions refusing now to permit myself the logical sanity given my situation. I called Sarah's home phone. I was utterly fed up with the idea of living in even a motorhome. I had long, long ago refused to dislike the violent streets I might rest my head on. Tar sealed dreams. There was, for me, a means to see the grimy, decaying interior as an obnoxious stage for homelessness.

This substitute for a suitcase contained my clothes and various work type necessities I needed when I got employed. I turned it upside down from the middle of the mattress and living rough painfully. I found the motorhomes insurance policy swiftly and looked impressed at the bed. Then with a deliberate movement, I lifted my fire starter in an empty envelope and quickly scanned the small side wall near the engine. The loose battered lid came off the lighter fluid, struck with care, and then without shifting position, I found my dwelling destroyed by an extreme fire blaze. My dirty brown winkle pickers, harking to Jackie Murder my favourite idol, I swung the ad-bag up on the carpet, blistering it with the cheap varnish I had paid $3 at the chemist in Durban. Then I picked up the swimming togs and a clean white T-shirt. I stepped into the environment. Now I was emotionally over the faded, peeling wallpaper and the downtown habitat, my hands placed on the stove with both hands. In spite of this urgency, I lit the bed and tossed in the alarm clock, my toiletries aflame.

Personal items, the deed, and an insurance policy accompanied my trip to the seven gates of the shades. I would look inside myself waiting as the motorhome burnt. Five hundred rand in cash could get me around the streets. This was the amount payable for insured value. I noticed my bed mattress, and I knew exactly that the plaster in the wall was going up like. And I watched some dark liquid cause the flame. I gazed for a moment at the stove until it was burning and acknowledged its great worth. The insurance contract was made out in the sum of five hundred rand. I could feel the heat of my chest, face, then I was certain, was the pain lying, waiting, resting in a backseat somewhere in the derelict pavement burial grounds? Warmth and happiness collected in my mind at the prospect of homelessness.

The insurance money would help. But who needs it? In fact, I was suddenly replacing the policy in its envelope with discreet secrecy. Quickly, I got my feet going, pulling on my tight-fitting T-shirt. I slid away, dreaming the motorhome was solid dirt. I knelt, escaped into the arid morning and with absolute conviction in my dreams. I was sure that I had not left something behind. I walked quickly out to the bus station across the roads and picked up pace with my ad-bag. It was absolutely necessary for me to be across town at the correct time, leaving for another urban environment, away from the motorhome when the fire was discovered, down the dirt road towards the city, the sight of the dense infrastructure. Moving swiftly for the last time in my life, travelling just beyond my broken dwelling reminded me that it was pure beauty living a life within the communal space of urban design. I felt no regret or guilt and closed the door in my subconscious, swapping humanness for the barbarism of a vulgar vagrant. I would just have to leave to lady luck my curiosity and desire to be certain that all went well. But to please myself, I glanced once more around the room, and I hated now had to be a dream itself. My grume left and stained no one but the burns masking it. I missed the report of the fire, and I realised I could reach a point that my presence could easily be the cause of more investigations from the insurance adjuster if anyone learned that I had taken essentials in my ad-bag before I went and disappeared. Opening that barrier in my mind, I hesitated and turned my head. I dared not wait and wanted nothing of the risk involved in reappearing. Remaining near the house for another minute overwhelmed me.

I didn't want to stir a muscle until I surpassed where the trees came close to the main road. I ducked into the waiting shelter. The ad-bag came with me when I left the house. There would certainly be questions. Even if all went exactly right, the guilt would be on my nasty face. Smoke shot into the sky. Under the kitchenette, curling smoke, a state of suspended decay and rather suddenly a tiny wisp of natural excitement. But I continued to stare at the shelters seats. My heart skipped a beat, then I drew in my breath sharply. The company agents asked about me, but the fire chief considered that the mattress burst into an open and consuming fire but lazily into the dead still air of my room. My heart pumped quietly for a time. I stood positively still as if I were in line at Hoyts Cinema. I now assume I have some need to hurry, and I moved as if I were in a trance, I started walking to the bus. In my mind, I was standing beside the bed, and I watched and waited for it to disintegrate. I was in the sadomasochistic navy, the armed forces of personal hate. No little conservative personality. I assume living in the gutter next to a cheap, ugly hotel in Durbans central districts would be the location for my minds love of legitimate vagrancy. I had often dreamt that I stayed there, living rough without negative effects. But at the present, I decided that I could give a moment to discovering my foul needs, achieving the bodily breaking but without the quiet nothingness of the countryside.

I would be delighted at this if the rubbish bins overflowed with filth. Their nourishing waste seemed so great to my feminine mind. Finding the pot of gold at the end of the rainbow without a regular job, I had actually dreamt all my life of getting by somehow and after a while, but I didn't want to think about that. Would I pay in advance for it? In the meantime, I had to eat. I have no need to look for a job. I was looked at scornfully by the elderly cross person at the inn. And I let the air dry my skin as I shaved my legs. Then depressing myself, I got out of my makeshift bed in the alleyway and went backwards falling into my bed. I closed my eyes and tried not to disturb the evil items in the streets. I could drift, and nobody would care. Concrete has a stuffy heat, and I bathed in the gloom of a hazy twilight Tophet. Durban, the city, and its millions of people would hide the shocking dreams I dream. In large cities, I could have absolute legitimacy, rocking me into a deep dreamless sleep from which I control the acts of hate. Now that I was free and on my own, I felt I should find a shower for five minutes. Kneeling under a dripping skip bin, I found the filthy water staining my skin irregularly. My hand, turned up, seemed brown, and my face camouflaged in a warping pattern. I felt refreshed after that, losing consciousness, but I was too tired to sleep. Cooling waves of relief and contentment soon arrived with the animal-like release of moral hindrances. I was clean. Directly into my open-air bathroom, I stood under a cold and smelly drip of liquid. Even if I chose to seek out another world, I was at last completely alone. Once, I was a working advert maker employed at the highest level of financing in London. I transubstantiated into a heavy mass of bodily bruised and grotesque soma. I was connected to vibrant madness. But this didn't matter because I could sleep rough, and with a hard concrete wall for a head rest, I would use the streets to project dreams. What happened to me was exactly the way I wanted it. I was sick of being forced to live, fitting in, and went out beside the hotel to get supper from the refuse down the road. I did not awaken until just before nightfall. Early in the evening, I decided to walk for a while and thought to myself plainly that I just wanted to be back in the world the way I had dreamt. The night auditor, departed quickly without looking at the alley. I would report her to the manager if she only ever would recognise the night life being homeless. The night auditor was a young male imitator who was paid five rand for a seven-day week plus tips. Her tits and ass cut down to fit the harder fake male shapes. I approached an exciting party 15 buildings away. The night auditor missed the refuse in the streets hidden bins. I was sure the girl-boy was gay, so I told myself the street is our temporary home and asked her if she would like to go eat. The bins are teeming with tainted morsels and liquid rubbish. The night auditor resided on the second floor for which she had to pay twenty a month. I felt dull as I opened my eyes. The room was tidy, except for the painted wooden floorboards. I stripped off all my clothes, pulled the top sheet back over a stained figure. That was why I had come to Durban in a very shocking manner. The streets were less crowded at this time of the crocodile season. The girl-boy began to speak. "Youd like to be up here with me sometimes as my guest, work out."

"Thanks. Id like to very much."

I want to keep in shape, and I knew I couldn't afford to be open about my wishes. She flicked out the lights and stood beside me, her mattress was good enough for us, but I was suddenly aware that the night auditor was standing much closer to me than was necessary, and her odour seemed heavy in the coolness of her room. I said nothing. She stayed in this position. Instead, I thought I began to wonder, but soon I became conscious of a subtle recognition. She stirred faintly, resting her arm on my thigh bone. I knew what she might set her heart on when her hand moved slowly, but I only relaxed now, making my mind an empty top and her body a piece of freshly-cured meat. Her inquisitive lips touched my belly and then my closed mouth, which she opened quickly with her tongue. After a while, the night auditor lay back and stretched out on her own side of the bed to rest. Immediately I got out of bed and went into the bathroom. I turned on the light over the black and white tile counter and gazed at my own reflection in the mirror. "You are a stinkhole," I said to myself to be taken off the streets by some housed employee.

But the experience wasnt after all without pleasure and a certain vile enjoyment. I feel satisfied now, my brain rolling over like the trees on a pathway. I went back to the alley by her place of work, missing the dripping bin cleaning I had days before. Wearing my swimming togs, I considered that at least I hadn't been roughed up by some female waster with a high voice and a fleshy body. I would never let such a person touch me. I was making the comparison in my mind, and this was the thing that most surprised me: The night auditor was a beautiful athletic type, and I had never had that. I thought recalling some abnormal masculine femininity, recalling Jackie Murder, my idol. The revelation left me a bit surprised and peculiarly in awe, but I don't think disgusted. My body was dreadfully sticky, so I decided to take a shower under some new leaking rubbish bin in the alleyway. I stood under its repugnant water and let it penetrate my body until I began to feel numb. Then I let the water ran off and stepped out into the artificial bathroom on the footpath. I wasnt startled because the night auditor half expected what she saw. Caleb sat on a stool and watched me, tossed a clean towel, which I caught with my working hand. I started to dry my hair. Neither of us spoke, but our eyes met, and they remained staring all the while I was drying myself. I wondered casually if I ought to feel self-conscious about someone like him watching me, but I decided that I didn't particularly mind. After all, she knew my body very well now, and she had no reason to be ashamed of my build, which was a perfectly formed, lean, and muscular female of 34. If the night auditor got some sort of enjoyment out of looking at me, that wasnt a crime. At last, they talked. "I hope I didn't shock or scare you," she said.

"Don't worry, you didn't. I took everything in stride."

"Im wrong. Maybe I should give you some advice, but I guess I was afraid of that. I don't know what I would do if you got up and clothed yourself. Probably nothing, but I wanted you so much so I might try to overpower you. I live a double life, of course, but you don't—"

"I don't," I answered, knowing this was the truth and knowing that the night auditor knew it too. I wanted to impress it upon her with the firmness in my voice.

"Here you go. That means you let me trap you."

"Don't be fooled, my friend."

Caleb Nembele lay and listened to me breathe. I was in a deep sleep beside him. It was that time just before dawn when the sky over the makeshift bedding and cardboard packing on Durbans ugly shocking streets was beginning to be streaked with light. She propped herself up on one elbow and stared at me. I was lying on my back on top of the wrinkled newsprint, plastic blanket, hats, and skirts. Caleb thanked fate silently and profusely for sending to her this beautiful young girl-boy with the stained face and rotten body broken by filth and nourished by liquid rubbish. This night with her had been supreme excellence. She appreciated and felt an unexpected pride she had been privileged to make love to the urban waste, this vagrant dreamer, yes, yes, trash believer. I was incapable of understanding why we couldn't subvert the lives of the rich, like two girls winning in a game of "chicken" with the wealthy people of South Africa. She sat up abruptly, and her eyes focused on me lying on my side, my smashed leg tucked up against my stomach and my arm folded across my chest. The sheet of plastic blanket was lying in a crumpled ball near my feet at the bottom of the cardboard, but

I didn't reach down and pull it up around my body. Caleb was afraid that if she woke me up, I would want to violently shock the streets with her instantly. She clad himself. She knew if I woke up seeing her still undressed, she would have to transgress Durbans loose moral customs. She didn't want that until it was time to clean up our invisible bodies. She didn't think she could relax on an empty stomach in the light of the afternoon. She wondered again if she had been a fool to sell her body this way, but she decided that any regrets were certainly erased by the warmth of the gutter, and she absolutely would not mind doing it again for the same consideration. It was realisable, when she thought of it, but she hadn't actually minded my body touching her because she thought I had such tight, hard flesh, not at all like the loose, flabby skin most women who had been attracted to her and pressed against her with desire shaking their bodies. She picked up her underwear from the floor next to their bedding, put them on, and went over to the rain pipe where her other clothes were and put on her tight T-shirt and kilt. She went into the alley in her masking tapped feet, opened the bin lid, and rinsed her mouth with some purified rubbish scum she found on it. She admitted to herself that she was very hungry. She knew there had to be a heap of tainted waste somewhere in the alley, and she decided to find herself some sustenance by cracking open the bins. She went down the beautiful concrete walkway to some skip containers. She found soiled nappies, vomit, liquefied fruit, and lots of paper partially and cleverly concealed behind an overheated microwave screen. She hadn't noticed last night and in one brick wall there was a cavity holding a bounty of horrid darkened rice. The microwave screen was from a model that sat on a countertop, was full of more trash fragments than she could remember. She likened the plentiful amount to her parents kitchen cupboards. Everything went as smoothly as if it had been rehearsed many times. There was not a single flaw in any of the scenes that were played during the rest of that rainy day. The two characters in the cast seemed oddly familiar with their parts, awaiting only the right moment to assume the roles. I had quietly and patiently waited back in our hotel alley for the unexpected, my dozy head resting on the concrete footway. When the call came, I didn't learn much from Sarah over the phone, except that she wanted to see me again and asked me to come back to her own sundowner encampment immediately. I took to moving on the overland rail because I knew this reunion was urgent. The homeless see the inner world with extreme vividness. I see Sarah, and she starts to sign tiredly, "Im sorry," speaking, "Im gonna return to work, if you are ever tempted to leave tell me."

"Do I do it to provoke you, girl? Im the queen of everything underground. Im my luv, Jackie Murder!"

"Go back to where you come from. You owe me. Im—"

"You taught us, Sarah. Think of all the fun youll have with my team of vagabonds. I will eat Durbans free food later with my girl, and you will just stop us three breaking our bodies. Look, bloodstained objects in some garbage department at a table I had previously reserved for three." She glared at me and went back into her rickety shelter, and I looked at her in total rage. "Why?" She yelled, "I'm beyond leaving!"

"You taught me!" I hissed back, losing sight of her. "Theres an honour code between the world, the sick and every other thing . . . You know the money doesnt help you. Theres still violence in the streets. And we could use the confusion. Its a vagrants town, girl!"

I knew there was nothing she could do to reverse the changes in her mind. I had her ultimately; she was an obstinate, self-centred woman who would probably get more pleasure out of hurting and crushing my loves than having me by her side. I was shocked with so much passion and rage at her that I knew it would be impossible for me to have a good time even if she retracted her decision and join our misfits eating Durbans tainted rubbish. I decided there was nothing left for me to do but go back to my makeshift bedding in my alley passageway. I felt that I didn't want to spend the long existence without more homeless allies next to me. I could become even alone if I returned to the alley where I would be discarded. What should I do? And almost at once, I knew, as if there had been a black widow subconsciously resting and waiting for the right moment to become known to me. It occurred to me that I should call the night auditor, and this seemed to be the most useful act in the hard streets. I saw the grey-blue telephone there on the pavement curb, and I didn't stop myself using it. Caleb hung up the phone, waiting for tied-up nights of wandering stars to her comforting bedding; she leaned and felt completely thrilled and updated her inner monologue. All she would think about was me; Id impart how perfect this place was going to be. She knew her eyes would tremble in joyous pain and bloody sweat. She quickly surveyed the room, some faded and derelict seating, which was pulled out at night for her bed, only placed without the pretence of being hidden from sight. The street room expanded to an open plan. But that was privileged and ideal. Changing the cushions into a bed only took her a minute, and then she went over to the rubbish bin and found some liquid scum to wash down her face. Staining her hands and wetting down her now-browned hair, she combed with much care, and after that, she rubbed a blemish off her neck. She wanted to look her very best for this occasion because it was no longer possible to ignore what she felt for me. She had acknowledged it this morning when she had seen me, looking comfortable, secure, and so handsome. She was in love with me. They would make love. There was a knock on the door. Caleb's reverie was abruptly shattered and replaced immediately with a strong physical desire that almost choked her as she opened the door and saw me standing there. But somehow she managed to grin and speak. "Hi, hi," he said. "Come on in."

I looked at her, and suddenly, she wanted an angry moment. Immediately, she regretted the impulse. She didn't understand what was wrong with her. "Heres the alcohol," she said as she stepped into the footway and handed the bottle to me. "Makes you high," she said. "Want a drink? Its really marvellous."

I let the water run for a minute, and I bit Caleb hard in the face. Slipping, our lips crushed together, filled with desire for pain. This was a beginning, hard clawing against her body, and I held her arm back behind her ankle. I was incapable of speaking. Awe shot down my spine. Our stained appendages pooled around dirty blood. Two girls fight to grow. My arm bent backwards, and a little black substance splashed against her nipple. Biting her, I cut it away, still attached, operating near her bleeding chest. The nipple hit the ground, causing the concrete to stain brown mess. Caleb was no longer afraid and appeared as if in a dreamlike state. She seemed relieved. Her awakening had come over her fully and made her heart and pulse beat furiously. My negative emotion now, I only felt fascination for traumatic revelation. I knelt on the bedding, and for a minute, my eyes met nothing but the night auditor standing above her. But she felt no moral guilt towards Caleb's body and a quick stirring of excitement like you have broken a body and relaxed to watch it bleed. "Look at me. Come on. Just open your eyes and look at me. Quickly," she said. "Turn out the lights."

I undressed her completely. She kept her eyes closed and her body limp as I readied some old metal keys I found on the payphone. Her body bent as it lay, wouldn't permit her to stand. Instead, I grabbed her waist and rolled her over on her back. Using the keys to cut a deep Liz into his eyebrow, I watched her face wrinkle, letting me teach her pain and have her bleed, sick back into her own mouth. Though she knew what aroused a kind of conscious dreaming, my animated hands scored a cut down her stained jaw. Her hands now fell on her bare skin. She felt great relief, and she reached up. Her arms and pulled me down, a sudden weight that gave her no warning of her new strength. I felt her pull my T-shirt out of my kilt, and I felt her hands on my body, wrecking my back. I made no effort to move or speak, even when we swam in silent streets. She thought ridiculous then with Caleb, bent under her body weight, which made her feel dead. "Its all right in a minute, mate."

She held her breath. She was amazed at herself behaving like this, but her mind seemed to have no moral limits. Her eyes opened automatically so I could see. "No." she said. "I want to look at you, and I want more pain."

When she heard me get up from the bed and strip, she crawled over on her stomach and for a long moment, said, "Nothing, Im going to shut my eyes for a minute."

Long after their bodies were exhausted and they had stopped loving to cut and break each others fresh femininity, they lay wide awake in bed, trying desperately to understand why she had to feel the way she did with this young woman whose name she did not even know. She felt complete enjoyment and total satisfaction.